SEASIDE BOOK CLUB

LOBSTER BAY BOOK 6

MEREDITH SUMMERS

CHAPTER ONE

"*M*ove it, or lose it."

Bunny Howard said the words out loud to herself as she snugged her thick wool sweater tighter and trudged down the beach, her shoes making imprints in the soft sand. At least that was what she'd read about staying young and active while aging. Bunny was about to turn seventy, and she intended to be the youngest seventy she could. "Seventy is the new fifty" was her motto.

Bunny loved her life. She had everything she could want and wanted to keep it that way. She had her independence and her creative endeavors, like crossword puzzles and painting, and she was hardly ever lonely because she had wonderful neighbors who were more like family. There was one thing she could use more of, though—mental activity. But that was where the new Lobster Bay Book Club came in. And that was where she was headed right now.

There would be plenty of mental stimulation as they discussed the protagonists and underlying themes of each book they read. Bunny could hardly wait to get started. They'd chosen a murder mystery by Edward Kingsley for the first book. She'd devoured the book in two days and couldn't wait to tell the group how she'd deciphered the clues in order to figure out the identity of the killer early on in the book.

In keeping with her health initiative, she'd parked her car in the public beach parking lot, which was fairly empty this time of year since it was the first week in October. Walking down the beach was always such a pleasant task, except maybe when it was windy and cold, like now. Not to mention it was getting dark. Bunny glanced behind her at the empty lot, envisioning how that might feel a little threatening when she had to walk back to her car after dark.

"No worries," she said out loud. "I'm sure I'll be fine."

Tides, the quaint seaside inn where the book club's first meeting was being held, came into view. The old Victorian was one of the oldest buildings on the beach and fit right in with its large turret, wide back deck, and widow's walk at the very top of the roof. Tables were still set up on the back deck for guests to enjoy break-fasts outside. It was early fall, and there were still some nice days left to eat outside while gazing at the ocean.

Lights were on inside, and she could see people moving about. Claire from Sandcastles Bakery was standing in the dining room. Hopefully, she'd brought some of her delicious pastries. Andie, one of the sisters who owned the inn, was stacking coffee mugs on the sideboard next to a big coffee urn. Some of Bunny's neighbors were there, too, including Sheila Donahue and Olga Svenson. Liz Weston, the new gal who had moved in next door to Bunny, was setting out some napkins and plates. She worked at Tides part-time, so she'd probably stayed on after work.

Bunny tucked the hardcover book she'd been carrying under her arm and paused at the bottom of the steps to the deck. Cooper, Jane's golden retriever, trotted over. His friendly face, with his golden fur and soulful brown eyes, gazed through the glass at her.

She paused, putting one hand on the side of the house for balance as she lifted her left foot to dump sand out of her shoe.

"Bunny? What are you doing back here? You could have come in the front." Jane, the other sister who ran the inn, opened the door for her.

Bunny nodded back toward the ocean. "I walked down the beach. Gotta get my steps in."

Cooper rushed out to escort her up the steps, and she bent to pet him as the smell of coffee and muffins tugged her inside.

"Bunny!" Emma Chamberlain turned from the corner where she'd been talking to Hailey Robinson. Emma was Bunny's neighbor and had recently become good friends with Hailey, who worked for Claire at Sandcastles Bakery. The two had bonded over being single mothers with preteen girls. "I would have given you a ride."

"Thanks. I actually parked in the public lot and walked down the beach." Bunny received Emma's hug a little awkwardly. Even though they were very close as neighbors, she did find Emma to be a little overenthusiastic in the hugging department. But it was hard to fault the girl with her bright blue eyes and zest for life.

"Walked down the beach, you say?" Olga Svenson peered at Bunny from over her reading glasses. "You go, girl! That's how I got to be so spry at my age. You have to keep moving."

Olga, another of Bunny's neighbors, was ninety going on thirty. She lived alone and refused to move despite her children practically begging. She did pretty well on her own, and everyone in the neighborhood looked out for her.

"I can give you a ride back to your car after if you want." Liz appeared at Bunny's side. She glanced out the doors toward the ocean. "It will be pitch-black by the time we're done."

"Thanks. I might take you up on that." Bunny tried to make it sound like she wasn't afraid of walking down the lonely beach alone in the dark, but she was secretly relieved.

Liz held out a tray loaded with little pieces of toast topped with basil, mozzarella, and grape tomato halves. "Have one."

Bunny grabbed a napkin then one of the hors d'oeuvres and popped it into her mouth. "Delish! Are the tomatoes from your garden?"

Bunny knew Liz's garden well since she'd helped plant and harvest it and was lucky enough to be able to take as much as she wanted.

"Yep, there are still a few last tomatoes left."

Hailey came to stand beside them. "Watch out for those weird-looking pastries." She whispered, pointing to a try of something that looked like orange Danish. "Claire is experimenting with recipes for fall, and those are sweet potato Danish." She made a face.

Bunny noticed the tray was still full, while the brownies beside it were going fast. "Should I have brought something?"

"Oh no! You know Claire—she always brings stuff from the bakery, and I just didn't want all the tomatoes to go bad. No one else brought anything. If we all did, there would be way too much food," Liz assured her.

"That's the thing about tomatoes. They all seem to ripen at once. And these were late bloomers," Bunny said as she edged toward the brownies.

"Okay! Everyone. Let's get the discussion going. Grab a plate of food and something to drink and follow me."

Jane led them to a cozy room in the back of the inn. Bunny had been to Tides a few times but mostly to the larger rooms in the front. This one had a large stone fireplace and window seats. Chairs were set in a circle, and small tables had been placed thoughtfully so everyone would have something to put their snacks on.

Bunny chose a chair near the tall windows that faced the ocean. To her left, a row of bookcases went halfway up the wall. They were loaded with leather-bound books, and she could practically smell the vanilla scent of their old, yellowed pages.

"What a great reading room." Olga made a slow circle around the room while nibbling on a cracker with cheddar cheese on it.

"It's one of my favorite rooms in the whole house. Dad was going to make it into a library." Jane smiled as her gaze traveled around the room, then her smile dimmed. "But that never came to be."

"Still could happen." Olga took a seat next to Emma.

"We have a lot of things to do here and a limited

budget, so it's at the bottom of our priority list. Maybe someday." Jane glanced at Andie, who had just bitten into the orange Danish and looked a bit surprised. Apparently, she hadn't gotten the warning. Jane frowned then held up her book. "Now then, what did you guys think of the book?"

"I thought it was a little scary." Olga glanced at the hardcover on the table next to her as if she were afraid it might come to life. Bunny hadn't thought the book overly scary. In fact, it had seemed quite mild to her.

"I thought it was fascinating. Especially the parts with the cat." Maxi plucked a grape off her plate.

A shadow near the door caught Bunny's eye. Was that someone lurking in the hall? Probably her overly active imagination. Anyway, shadowy hall lurkers went hand in hand with mystery book discussions.

She turned her attention back to the conversation as each person said a little bit about the book.

"I thought it was nice," Hailey mumbled.

"Nice?" Claire squinted at her. "There was a murder."

"Oh, I know but... umm..."

"Wait. Did you even read it?" Andie teased good-naturedly.

Hailey's face turned red. "Okay. Busted! I didn't have time. It's hard with Jenn always wanting to be driven here and there."

There were murmurs of sympathy all around.

"It's okay," Jane assured her. "I'm sure you could use a night out."

Hailey blew out a breath. "You can say that again. Gramps is watching her, and they enjoy their alone time too."

"What about the characters?" Jane got the conversation back on track. "I love Abigail Childs."

"Didn't Franny Parker remind you of Ellen at the library? With those gigantic glasses and big eyes."

Everyone laughed.

Bunny glanced out into the hallway again. She was sure someone was there, but why? The room was in the back, so the hall didn't lead anywhere else. Were they listening in?

"The killer was a big surprise. Did anyone else figure it out?" Emma glanced around the room at the others.

Bunny waited just a tad to see if anyone else had. Maybe her skills of deduction weren't as great as she thought. But everyone just shook their head.

"I did. And early on too."

"You did?" Liz looked impressed. "How did you figure it out?"

Bunny was practically bursting with pride. "I followed the clues. Like the hole in the garden? The author led you to believe it was for a shrubbery, but I knew it was to hide the murder weapon!"

"How did you know that?" Claire asked.

Bunny opened her book to the section where she'd put a green sticky note. "In chapter five, the landscaper brings five shrubs and plants them next to the driveway."

"Oh, gosh, I didn't even notice that." Andie passed around a tray of cookies.

"And there was also the clue at the farmers market," Bunny said.

"You mean the green tomatoes?" Olga asked.

"That was a red herring," Bunny said. "But the disruption at the local honey stand was the clue."

"You're really good at this, Bunny. Maybe you should be a detective." Emma's compliment practically made Bunny blush.

"Oh, it's just a matter of deduction." Bunny tried to sound humble. She was going to add that anyone could do it if they paid attention to the details, but she was distracted by more movement in the hallway. She craned her neck to see around Jane, who was blocking her view of the hall.

"What I don't get is how did the killer dispose of the body so easily?" Claire was trying to pass around the tray of sweet potato Danish, but everyone was claiming to be full.

"Oh, that was easy." Bunny leaned forward as if about to reveal a big secret, and everyone else leaned in too. She lowered her voice. "You see, the killer simply went to the site beforehand and—"

Creak!

Heads jerked toward the sound in the hallway.

Jane leapt up from her chair.

"Hello? Can I help you... oh, Mr. Smith! What can I do for you?"

"Err... sorry. I... umm... Someone said there would be coffee, and I wanted a cup." The voice came from the hallway, and Bunny tilted to the right to look around Jane so she could see who it belonged to.

"It's in the dining room. I'll show you." Jane put her book on her chair and hurried into the hall.

The hall was only dimly lit by a wall sconce, but right before they turned to go to the dining room, Bunny caught a glimpse of Mr. Smith. He looked to be in his mid to late forties. He was average height, with dark hair cut short and beady dark eyes. Okay, she couldn't actually see his eyes, but she'd bet money they were beady.

Bunny turned to the group as Mr. Smith and Jane disappeared down the hall. "Coffee? Does anyone else think that's a little odd?"

Olga raised her mug filled with coffee. "Not me."

"He was probably really looking for the pastries," Sally said.

"He keeps strange hours and drinks a lot of coffee. It's not that unusual," Liz said.

Jane returned, and they continued to discuss the book, but Bunny was only half paying attention. Something about Mr. Smith had her concerned. If her intuition was correct—and it usually was—then Mr. Smith was up to no good. But what was he up to?

There was only one way to find out. She'd already proven that her skills of investigation were superior when it came to book detecting, and now she was going to prove they were superior in real life. Bunny was going to find out what Mr. Smith was up to, no matter what it took.

*B*unny took Liz up on her offer of a ride to her car after the book club. She didn't want to walk down the dark beach, but she also wanted to pump Liz for information about Mr. Smith.

"It's kind of weird that there's only one person staying at Tides, don't you think?" Bunny asked.

"Not this time of year. Jane said hardly anyone comes because it's too late for beachgoers and too early for leaf-peeping." Liz chewed on her bottom lip. "I guess you could say it's unusual to even have *one* guest since it's off-season."

"Huh." Bunny added that to her list of suspicions. "Mr. Smith does seem unusual. Especially the way he was lurking in the hallway during our book discussion."

Liz looked over at her. "Lurking? He was just looking for the coffee urn. I'd mention to him earlier that we would have coffee and snacks."

"I think I saw him standing in the hallway for a while, and everything was set up in the dining room. You'd think he would have seen it in there."

Liz shrugged. "He doesn't seem to be overly observant."

"Really? What is he like? Why is he in town?"

Liz laughed. "Is this an inquisition? He's quiet and mostly stays in his room. Though I have seen him go out to the beach a few times. It's still nice enough for walking."

"Is he visiting relatives?"

"I really have no idea. I only work a few days a week. He's polite. I'll tell you that." Liz frowned. "Though I do wonder why he is here. He seems lost in thought and very private. Maybe he's recovering from a death of a loved one or something."

Or planning a murder. That probably takes a lot of thought. At least it did for the killer in the book they'd just read.

"Don't you think Smith is kind of a common name?" Perfect to use for someone who wanted to hide their real identity. "Did he pay in cash?"

Liz glanced at her. "Bunny, I think you might have gotten too involved in our mystery book. Real life isn't like books. Smith is a common name. Tides was bound to get some guests named Smith that pay in cash. I'm sure Andie saw his license when she checked him in."

"Of course. Silly of me." Bunny sat back in the seat. She didn't want Liz to think she was a foolish old lady. She decided to change the subject. "Did you try the sweet potato Danish that Claire brought?"

Liz made a face. "I didn't have the heart to tell her they weren't that good. I should have, though. She said she was trying them out on us. It's good that she's trying different recipes for the bakery."

"I agree. I love everything she carries there, but it's always fun to have something different. Maybe if she put more sugar in them."

"At least she didn't try to make us test out the dog biscuits that she's added to her repertoire." Liz laughed.

"I don't know. Cooper sure seemed to like them."

"I'll follow you back," Liz said as she pulled up next to Bunny's Volkswagen.

They lived next to each other, so of course they'd be driving the same route. Did Liz think Bunny was worried about driving in the dark? Maybe her eyes weren't as good as they used to be, but she could still drive fine! Still, Bunny appreciated that Liz wanted to keep her safe, so she thanked her and got into her car. She made sure to pull out first so Liz could see for herself that she had no problem navigating after sunset.

As she drove home, her thoughts turned to the mysterious guest at Tides. What should be the next step in her investigation? Maybe she should take another look at her book to see how the detective in the book went about investigating and figure out if she could do something similar.

CHAPTER TWO

*C*laire arranged the dog biscuits up in the display case carefully. She had a special section for them and was careful to keep them away from the human pastries. People seemed to get upset about that even though every ingredient in the biscuits was perfectly safe for human consumption and probably healthier than the sugar-laden pastries she was known for.

"I sold a ton of dog biscuits yesterday." Hailey breezed in, wrapping the strings of her white apron around her waist and grabbing the coffee carafe. The earthy aroma of dark roast swirled around her, mingling with the sweet scent of muffins and cakes baking in the kitchen out back. "You're going to have to think of a name for them. People keep saying 'the dog biscuit thingies.'"

"I did that last night after the book club." Claire held up a sign she'd made on her printer last night. She'd had to call her daughter, Tammi, to help figure out the right fonts and so on, but Claire was proud of the way the sign had come out. It looked professional. "Beach Bones. What do you think?"

"It's catchy." Hailey slid out from behind the counter to top off the coffee mugs of the customers seated at the tables. It was only eight thirty, and the murmur of early-morning conversation and clinking of spoons against porcelain mugs filled the space. Claire's heart swelled at the number of customers already inside the café. There were even a few brave souls sitting at the outside tables, bundled in sweaters, with dogs at their feet.

The bakery was Claire's pride and joy, a dream she hadn't been brave enough to bring to fruition until after her divorce. That had been years ago, and everything was going perfectly for her now. She had a thriving business, her grown daughter was doing well, and she had even forgiven her husband for dumping her for a younger woman.

Sure there had been some blips, like when she'd thought the new bread store opening across the street was a threat to Sandcastles, but her fears had been unfounded. And now that she was dating the owner of the bread store, Rob, well... things were better than ever.

With Hailey minding the customers, Claire went out back and grabbed some fresh muffins for the case. She was just putting the last one in when Sam Campbell came in the door.

Sam was in his early seventies, tall and thin, with a thick head of snowy hair, a prominent nose, and a kind way about him. Sam used to come with his wife, Jean, most mornings. The couple had practically vibrated with life, always happy and talkative. They would sit at the corner table for hours with Sam, entertaining people with stories of his exploits as a police detective.

But then Jean got sick. Their visits had become less frequent, less cheerful. She'd passed two years ago, and Sam had stopped coming. It was only recently that he'd returned, now with a bloodhound mix named Dooley, who was now tied up on the post outside that Claire had put out expressly for her customers to tie out their dogs if they were just popping in to buy something. Dogs weren't allowed inside, but the outdoor seating at Sandcastles had become very popular with dog owners. That had sparked the idea of branching out into gourmet dog biscuits.

Sam still seemed sad. His posture was stooped, almost as if he were trying to cave in on himself and disappear. His complexion was sallow. His blue eyes no longer sparkled with mischief like they used to. He was here, though, and that was something at least.

Claire gave him one of her biggest smiles, wishing

her happiness were contagious and could spread it to him. "Hey, Sam, what can I get you?"

"How about a corn muffin and one of those new biscuits for Dooley?" Sam turned to look out the door at Dooley almost as if to reassure himself the dog—who was staring into the store, eyes locked on Sam—was still there.

"Coming right up. Coffee?"

"Yes, black please. Just a small. No, make it a medium. Dooley and I might sit a spell on that bench by the beach."

"That sounds nice." Claire busied herself getting Sam's order.

"I think Dooley would like it," Sam said as if any enjoyment he could get out of life was over and he was only doing it for the dog.

She was glad to hear he was at least going to sit at the beach. Sam and Jean had walked the beach and the Marginal Way—the popular path that ran along the edge of the ocean cliffs—almost every day. Sam had given that up since her passing. But maybe sitting would lead to walking, and maybe that would lead to more enjoyment for Sam.

"Have a great time." Claire handed him the bag. "I put an extra biscuit in for Dooley."

"Thank you." Sam almost smiled as he took the bag and shuffled out the door.

Claire watched him unhook the dog and start

down the street. Dooley had been a gift from Sam's son, Brad. He'd thought taking care of a dog would give Sam a purpose, but watching the two of them and the way Dooley obviously slowed himself down to keep pace with Sam and kept glancing up at the man, she had a feeling it was really Dooley taking care of Sam.

As she watched them disappear down the street, another person caught her eye. Wasn't that the strange man from Tides?

She craned her neck to look closer. Yes, it was Mr. Smith. Kind of a weirdo, really. Bunny had said he'd been lurking in the hallway during the book club meeting. Claire wasn't so sure she believed that, but he was an odd one. Not very friendly, according to Jane.

He was walking down the sidewalk with a purpose, not at all like a tourist on vacation. She wondered where he was in such a hurry to get to.

*B*unny had stayed up late, thinking about Mr. Smith and how she should go about figuring out exactly what he was up to. She decided to do what the amateur sleuth in her mystery book would do: follow him.

She'd risen at the crack of dawn. The lack of sleep and early wake-up time didn't make her tired. In fact, the opposite had happened. The prospect of investigating something revitalized her and gave her energy.

She'd had to skip her morning painting session. She hated to do that. Painting was important to her, but this took precedence. She also hadn't been able to bring muffins over to Liz like she did four or five times a week. That was okay—she'd do that later this afternoon so she could pump Liz for more information about Smith.

She filled a thermos with coffee and drove past Tides before stopping a little ways down the street from the entrance. She parked under a low-hanging oak tree branch, hoping her car would blend in.

Unlike in the book, Mr. Smith did not zip right out of the entrance as soon as Bunny parked. She waited a few hours and was just about to give up when a car pulled out with Mr. Smith at the wheel. *Bingo!*

She followed several car lengths behind, just like the detective in the book. When he pulled into a spot downtown, Bunny pulled in a few spots away. At first she was nervous. There weren't many people out at eight forty-five, unless she counted the gang over at Sandcastles getting their morning coffees and Danishes. She was afraid Mr. Smith would notice her, but he didn't even glance in her direction as he locked his car. *Who locks their car in Lobster Bay?*

No one did. In Bunny's mind, that was further proof that he was of a suspicious nature and up to something.

He started down the sidewalk along the row of stores. She scrunched down in the seat and opened the newspaper she'd brought as a disguise. She slid it up to cover the bottom of her face, peeking up above it through her large-framed sunglasses every so often to keep her eye on the suspect.

Mr. Smith walked past the candy store with its pink-and-green awning and pyramids of fudge in the window, past the framing store where she'd had her ancestor's Civil War discharge papers that Andie had given her framed, past the jewelry store with its display of diamonds twinkling in elegant deep-purple velvet, and straight into the hardware store. *Very curious.*

About twenty minutes later, he came out holding a large bag. Bunny scrunched out of sight again as he made a beeline for his car. He was walking fast and acting almost as if he didn't want anyone to see him. Or was that her imagination?

As far as she knew, the hardware store only had tools and home improvement items. *What in the world would someone vacationing at an inn need with home improvement items or tools?*

She was about to pull out after him when she noticed the hunched-over man and his dog lurking around her car. Was he watching her?

She craned her neck to look at him in the side-view mirror. No, he wasn't watching her. The dog had just stopped to sniff something. But she didn't want to draw attention to herself, so she stayed put until they lumbered of toward Beach Street.

Luckily, she could still see Mr. Smith's car going slowly down Main Street. She pulled out, taking care to stay far enough behind, excitement thrumming in her veins. She was really on to something. And she was the only one who suspected him. With any luck, she could catch him before he did any harm and save someone from a terrible fate. *How's that for being useful!*

But it wasn't going to be today, because he went straight back to Tides.

Bunny drove past and took the back route home. Maybe she could still catch Liz at home and ask her some questions about the suspect. Besides, she'd finished off almost the whole thermos of coffee and really had to pee.

"*S*he gave me an extra biscuit for you," Sam said to Dooley.

He'd been doing that a lot lately—talking out loud to the dog. Funny thing, he almost felt like the dog was answering using some sort of silent communication technique. Like right now, he was looking up at Sam, one floppy ear tilted slightly and an eager look in his eye as if asking if he could have one of them now.

"Maybe when we get to the beach. We'll drive down

to the lot if you don't mind." It was only a ten-minute walk to the beach, but this time of year, the parking lot would be empty, and Sam hadn't walked that long in a while.

He felt a pang of guilt, knowing Dooley was dying for a longer walk, but Sam usually ran out of energy and enthusiasm after a few blocks. He was working his way up to it for Dooley's sake, though. And maybe a little for Jean too. She was the one who'd always insisted they walk one more block or to the next corner on the Marginal Way or just a little farther down the beach. She'd said it would help them live longer. It hadn't worked out so well for her. She wouldn't approve of Sam's lack of walking, but maybe he didn't want to live longer.

Dooley whined, as if sensing Sam's thoughts.

"Ah, don't worry. I won't leave you alone."

Most days, Sam wouldn't even get out of bed if it weren't for Dooley. Before Dooley, he had lain in there until noon a few days. But now, Dooley jumped up there at seven thirty every morning. Sam knew he had to get up to feed the dog and take him out. Dooley was depending on him, so he forced himself to get up.

That was getting easier lately, and he'd even started venturing downtown and taking the dog to the beach —things he hadn't done since Jean died. He wasn't sure if he liked it or not. It felt hollow and empty, like something was missing. Of course he missed Jean, but it was more than that. It was like he didn't have a purpose.

Dooley woofed and sniffed a pile of something gooey on the sidewalk. Sam's attention drifted to a parked car. It was a pale-blue Nissan, and a woman sat inside. She was reading a newspaper. How odd. *Who does that in a car?*

No, not exactly reading... He slowed down. Now that was very strange—she was scrunched down inside, peering over the paper as if canvassing the street. And she was wearing ridiculously large sunglasses. It reminded him of a comical version of all the stakeouts he'd been on when he was a detective.

Feelings of those times came flooding back. The excitement of the chase. The mental stimulation of following the clues to catch a dangerous criminal. The feeling that he was doing something useful, something good for society. But those days were long gone. There wasn't much to feel useful about anymore. Except Dooley.

Dooley tugged the leash, and Sam started walking again. "You know what, boy? Maybe we'll walk to the beach today instead of taking the car."

Dooley's tail wagged faster, and he picked up the pace.

CHAPTER THREE

*J*ane was bringing the last of the dishes from the book club meeting out to the kitchen when the front door of Tides opened and Mr. Smith came in. He started for the stairs then, upon noticing her, stopped short.

"Good morning! Were you out walking the beach? It's a bit chilly but gorgeous for a walk." Jane glanced out toward the ocean, where sunbeams bounced off cobalt waves.

He held up a shopping bag, barely making eye contact with her. "Had to pick some things up."

"Well, maybe later you can walk. It will be warm in the afternoon." Jane tried to keep the cheery tone in her voice even though Mr. Smith was already heading toward the stairs.

Liz came into the foyer, carrying a pile of freshly

laundered sheets and pillowcases. Jane had been having her do some of the chores that had piled up during the busy season since there was only one guest for her to see to at the moment.

"He sure is a strange one," Liz whispered after his door clicked closed.

"You can say that again. Seems very solitary and a little bit sad. I bet there's a story there." Jane continued on toward the kitchen, and Liz followed.

"Bunny thinks he's up to something." Liz put the laundry on the long pine table and started folding.

Jane turned from the sink. "What would he possibly be up to?"

Liz shrugged. "Beats me. You know Bunny—her imagination is very active."

Jane laughed. She really liked Bunny with her messy, silver-threaded auburn curls and fun attitude, and she had to admit it was a little weird that Mr. Smith had been in the hallway like that at the book club meeting.

"What's his first name, anyway? I keep calling him *Mr.* Smith. Seems very formal."

Jane squinted to remember. He'd filled out the forms online, shown her some credentials when he checked in, and paid in cash. She tried to picture the card he'd shown her. *Was it his license?* She couldn't remember. "I think it's Reginald."

"You mean our one and only guest?" Brenda the

cook turned from the stove she'd been cleaning. "He's not weird. He's very polite."

Brenda had been the cook at Tides for decades and insisted on making breakfast even though there was only one guest. Sometimes she even insisted when there were no guests. Brenda was more like family than an employee, though, and Jane loved having her around. Plus, she cooked a mean breakfast.

"You've spoken to him?" Jane was surprised. As far as she knew, the man mostly stayed in his room. He'd certainly never tried to be friendly to Jane.

"Yeah. Came down for breakfast yesterday. Hearty appetite on that one." Brenda beamed. Anyone who appreciated her breakfasts was just fine in her book.

"He never says much to me," Liz said.

"Guess I've got the magic touch," Brenda joked.

"Have you seen Andie?" Jane asked Brenda. "I thought she was going to meet us here."

"She was here earlier with Mike, but she left," Liz said.

Jane frowned. *Why would Andie and Mike be together?* Her sister and boyfriend were good friends, but she didn't think they hung out together. *And why would neither one of them stop by to see me?* "Are you sure she was with Mike?"

Liz looked up from her folding, her brows rising slightly at the look on Jane's face. "I thought so. Maybe I was wrong?" Liz glanced at Brenda for confirmation.

"I didn't see either one of them. The bread delivery came, though. Maybe you thought Eddie was Mike. Kind of looks similar." Brenda gave the stove another swipe.

That was probably it. *Though why would Andie be with the bread guy?* She had said she would come early to get some of her work done.

"She mentioned something about meeting us at Sandcastles." Liz glanced at the clock.

Brenda turned from the stove, noting Liz's gaze. "Speaking of which, aren't you two supposed to be there now? I'll watch over the place. Not much happening here." Brenda made shooing motions with her hands. "Go. I'll finish up."

*C*laire brought the tray of experimental fall-themed pastries out from the back and hurried to the table where her friends were gathered with their coffees.

"Specially made just for you guys." She set down the tray and took a seat eagerly watching the expressions on everyone's faces.

Jane looked a bit skeptical, her blue eyes lingering on each pastry, a line forming between her brows as if she were assessing what was in them.

Maxi was more eager. Her hair, now streaked with

white, was in a long ponytail that slid over her shoulder as she reached for a cinnamon cruller.

Andie gnawed on her bottom lip, her hazel eyes glittering, a whisper of long dark hair falling out of the bun atop her head as her hand hovered over the cider donuts.

"Are these all pumpkin and spices?" Liz pointed to the tray.

"Yep. Some are from the recipes you gave me." Claire pointed to the pumpkin-raisin muffins in the center.

"Looks delicious." Liz reached for one.

"What's this?" Jane pointed to a slice of cake with white frosting.

"Carrot cake with cream cheese frosting. I grated the carrots fresh myself." Claire watched with pride as each one of them ate their pastry and made num-num noises.

"So, they're all good? Should I add them to my offerings for the fall season?" Claire gestured toward the glass cases, where her baked goods, including the sandcastle-shaped cakes that the bakery was known for, were on display.

"The crullers are great. I'd add those." Maxi nodded, and the others nodded in agreement.

"But maybe not those sweet potato Danishes from the book club meeting." Jane grimaced, her voice soft.

Claire frowned. "No one liked those? I noticed hardly any were eaten."

"Sorry." Maxi reached for a molasses cookie. "But looks like everything here is great."

"Thanks." Claire wasn't upset about the sweet potato Danish. That had been an experiment. After all, that was what it was all about. Some of them didn't come out very good while others hit it out of the park. Like her dog treats. People really seemed to love them. In fact, a small crowd was gathering around the case that held them right now.

"Aren't these cute?" a woman in thick glasses said.

"Are they for people or dogs?" Her husband's face was almost pressed to the glass.

"Beach Bones. That sounds familiar," the lady next to him mused.

The first woman pushed her glasses up on her nose. "Has a good ring to it."

Perfect! Her name was familiar, with a good ring to it. That was just what she wanted. Except by "familiar," she hoped the woman meant it sounded comfortable and not like something from a famous brand. She made a mental note to call Tammi and ask her about researching trademarks. She didn't think anyone else had used that name for a dog biscuit, but one could never be too careful.

"How is your mysterious guest today?" Maxi's eyes

twinkled. "Do you really think he was creeping around last night?"

"Of course not." Jane waved her hand dismissively.

"That's just Bunny. She's creative even with her imagination," Liz said. "Brenda said the guy is really nice. He's probably just shy."

"Bunny is a character. She was a big help when I was stuck with painter's block." Maxi cut a pumpkin-spice muffin in half and glanced down at Cooper, who was sitting at Jane's feet.

"He doesn't need a muffin, Max," Jane said.

Everyone loved to give Cooper treats, and Jane was diligent about keeping him healthy.

"I think Mr. Smith is just a regular guy. Saw him going into the hardware store this morning, just like a normal person." Andie sipped her coffee.

"Oh, is that where you went off to?" Jane asked. "Did you need something for Tides there?"

"Oh no. I wasn't in the store. I was… Well, I had some errands. For the antiques store." Andie focused on rooting through the sweetener packets in a small basket in the middle of the table.

Claire thought she might be avoiding eye contact with Jane, but she could have been wrong. Maybe it was a sister thing she wasn't privy to.

"What would he be doing in the hardware store?" Claire asked.

"Maybe he's making some repairs to his room," Liz joked.

"How nice would it be if all the guests did that?" Jane mused.

"How is business at the shop?" Claire asked Andie, who had recently moved back to town and opened an antiques store.

"Great. Now that Liz is helping out at Tides, I have more time for house calls, which means I get to root around in creepy attics and spider-filled basements." The thought didn't appeal to Claire, but the look on Andie's face indicated it was one of her favorite activities.

"And the painting, Maxi? Any new masterpieces?"

Maxi laughed, a blush tinging her cheeks. She'd just completed a series of pet portraits, including one of Claire's cat, Urchin, and one of Cooper. "I'm working on a series of paintings looking at the ocean from different vantage points on the Marginal Way, and I have a pet portrait for Wendy Martinelli at Tall Pines."

Tall Pines was the assisted-living complex where Jane and Andie's mother, Addie, lived. That reminded Claire... "Don't let me forget to give you some chocolate chip muffins for Addie." She'd already put some in a bag, which was sitting in the kitchen.

"That's so nice of you," Jane said. "I'm heading over to visit her after this, so it's perfect timing."

"Did anyone get the new book for the book club

yet?" Jane asked. They'd chosen another mystery to read for next month's meeting.

"I have it on my Kindle," Liz said. "Bunny had hers in her mailbox already last night."

Maxi scrunched up her face. "I need a real book, so I ordered the paperback."

"I'm looking forward to reading it and to the next meeting," Andie said.

Claire nodded. "We all are."

"Especially Bunny," Liz said. "Let's just hope she doesn't take this mystery stuff too much to heart. She's already starting to get overly suspicious of your guest."

Jane laughed. "She is, but I'm sure it's all just talk. Bunny would never do anything crazy, and I'm glad she has something to keep her mind occupied."

CHAPTER FOUR

*B*unny dipped her smallest brush into the puddle of white-with-a-touch-of-cerulean-blue paint and leaned forward. She dabbed a spot on the canvas and then blended it in with quick strokes. She stood back to admire the work. It was a close-up of a pile of shells on the beach and looked almost like a photo. She was grateful that her eyesight was still good enough to make those fine details. It should be—she took enough bilberry extract and ate tons of carrots.

But the shells in the painting weren't quite right. She needed to add something in, something different. She liked to paint from real objects, and she made a mental note to check the low-tide schedule. There was a little beach off the Marginal Way near the small lighthouse that was a great place to find shells at low tide. The receding tide exposed rocks in the sand where starfish, crabs, and snails could be found. Once in a while, she'd run across a sea urchin. Looking for sea life around the rocks was one of her favorite pastimes, and if she found some interesting things to paint, all the better.

A car pulling in next door caught her attention. Liz was home! She put the brush in her mason jar of turpentine and hurried into the kitchen, where a loaf of fresh zucchini bread sat waiting on the counter. She'd baked it with the last of the zucchini from Liz's garden.

After placing the zucchini bread into a towel-lined basket, she grabbed cream cheese out of the fridge and headed on the well-worn path from her slider to Liz's kitchen door.

Liz answered with a welcoming smile. "That looks delicious. I just came from Sandcastles, though. I might have gone overboard sampling Claire's fall pastry line. But I can take this for later."

Bunny handed over the basket, and Liz invited her in. With the two of them, it was more about the company than the food.

At the sight of the kitchen, Bunny's eyes widened. The top cabinets had their doors open, and all the dishes were gone. The house had been Liz's childhood home, and she'd just moved in. It was outdated, and Bunny knew Liz intended to upgrade, but she hadn't realized she was doing it this soon. "Are you getting new cabinets?"

"I think so." Liz placed two mugs of tea on the table. "I was going to just replace the old Formica counters, but the guy that came out said it would make sense to do the cabinets at the same time, so…"

"Yeah, sounds like the smart move. It's going to be like a whole new place." Bunny looked around, feeling a little nostalgic. She'd known Liz's parents since they were around the same age and had spent quite a bit of time in this house before Liz moved in. She'd been especially close to Liz's father, Frank, after his wife died. But now Frank was gone, too, and she was getting close to Liz. Bunny never had children, and Liz was becoming like a daughter to her.

"Yeah, new but still familiar and comfortable." Liz gestured for Bunny to sit.

"So, what's the hubbub at Sandcastles? Did you guys discuss the book club and our little lurker?"

Bunny could hardly believe how lucky she was to be able to segue into asking about Mr. Smith so easily. She'd spent a considerable amount of time contemplating how she would broach the subject without sounding like a silly, gossiping old lady.

Liz raised a brow. "Are you still thinking about him? Brenda said he was really nice."

"That's what they said about Ted Bundy."

"Bunny! You don't really think the guy is a serial killer, do you?" Liz looked as if she were concerned about Bunny's mental health.

"No, of course not." Bunny waved her hand as if that were the farthest thing from her mind. *Maybe a thief or someone with a specific victim in mind, but certainly not a serial killer.* "He's just a little mysterious, and it makes me curious is all."

"Jane did find it odd that he was in the hardware store."

"Indeed. What was he there for?"

"Don't know. Andie saw him. He did bring a bag back to the inn but went straight to his room."

Bunny nodded and sipped, not admitting that she'd also seen Mr. Smith in the hardware store.

Bunny reached for a piece of zucchini bread that Liz had placed out along with the cream cheese. "Have you noticed him doing anything unusual?"

"Mr. Smith? No. He just stays in his room."

"Well, that seems unusual. Tourists typically go out and about. See the sights."

"He might have just needed alone time or something. You never know what people are going through, and some people take a trip to have alone time."

Bunny thought back to when her husband had died. She remembered going around in a fog while the rest of the world carried on around her as if nothing had happened.

"True. I mean, it's not like anyone found murder weapons or kill lists in his room while cleaning it." Bunny tried to sound like she was joking, but she could only hope Liz would mention something that Bunny would see as a clue.

"Of course not! Well, he asked not to have cleaning service, which, now that you mention it, is kind of odd…"

"Uh-uh." Who wouldn't want cleaning services? Someone with something to hide—that was who. "No weird noises coming from his room or nighttime excursions?"

"Jane didn't mention anything like that. I haven't seen or heard anything, but I'm not there much since it's off-season."

"You might want to check his trash, just in case."

"For what?"

"You never know! Look at what happened in our book club book."

"But that's just a book. It's not real life." Liz's brow furrowed. "Though I guess if you add up everything, it is odd."

Bunny sat back and smiled. At least she wasn't the only one who thought Mr. Smith was suspicious, because judging by the look on Liz's face, now she thought so too.

CHAPTER FIVE

*a*s assisted-living facilities went, Tall Pines was one of the best. It had friendly staff, expert medical care, wonderful activities for the residents, and great meals, and the rooms were like a posh hotel but with your own personal items and furniture.

Jane's mother, Addie, had been there for several months. Jane had been reluctant to move her there at first. Her instinct had been to care for her mother at home. But Addie's dementia meant Jane also had to take over running Tides, and doing both had become impossible. Tall Pines was a much better place for her, and she was thriving.

Cooper was a frequent visitor at Tall Pines. The management encouraged dogs, as it always seemed to please the residents, and Mike usually brought him once a week. Cooper loved car rides, so he was excited when

Jane brought him with her. When she parked in the lot, he knew exactly where he was and walked beside her to the front door.

Jane greeted the receptionist and then unleashed Cooper, letting him run down the hall ahead of her to Addie's room.

"Cooper! Are you back again so soon?" Addie smiled as the dog rushed to her. Addie always remembered Cooper, even if she did get Jane confused with her sister sometimes. Jane stepped into the room, which had been decorated with all of her mother's favorite things from the blue-and-white wedding ring quilt her grandmother had made to the bird figurines that had been gifts from her father to the furniture she'd had in her room at Tides.

"Well, it has been almost a week, Mom." Jane hadn't brought Cooper the last two times. She usually visited at least every other day, but mostly every day.

"Not you, dear. Mike was here with Coop yesterday." Addie pressed her lips together and looked up at the ceiling. "Or was it earlier today?"

He was? Cooper had initially been Mike's dog, but when his living circumstances had almost forced him to give up the dog, Jane had taken him in at Tides. Now that she and Mike were an item, they shared Cooper. He had taken Cooper yesterday, but he didn't mention coming to visit Addie. Her mother was probably confused about timing.

Jane held out the bakery bag. "Claire sent these."

"Isn't she sweet! Did she make them in that culinary school?" Addie reached her weathered hand into the bag and pulled out a muffin. "Nice job. She must be learning a lot."

Jane didn't correct her. Claire had gone to culinary school, but that was years ago. Addie's memory wasn't always cohesive.

"Did Mike get his sizes?" Addie asked.

"Sizes?"

"Measurements maybe. You know. Wait. Is it your birthday, dear? I didn't get you anything."

"It's not today, Mom. Don't worry. There's plenty of time."

"Oh. Phew." Addie bit into the muffin, spilling crumbs down her shirt. "Oh, look at me! What a mess!"

Claire had provided napkins, and Addie pulled one out. Then as if just remembering her manners, she tilted the bag toward Jane. "Would you like a muffin?"

"No thanks. I'm full." She'd eaten more than her share at Sandcastles.

"I'll save it for later." Addie winked and slid the bag into a drawer. Jane made a mental note to remove it before she left. Addie would forget it was in there.

"Anyway, I had a lovely chat with Mike." Addie looked down at the dog. "And you, too, Cooper. Mike is a good catch for you."

"I know." Jane did know, but something about the

way her mother said that lent her to believe that something strange was going on concerning Mike.

Liz had said Andie was with Mike this morning, and now her mom seemed to think Mike had been here asking about measurements. *Could it all be a coincidence?*

There was one way to find out. She had plans to meet Mike for a late lunch at their favorite restaurant, and she'd simply ask him.

CHAPTER SIX

*S*am broke the biscuit into four pieces and tossed one at Dooley, who caught it deftly. Dooley smiled and wagged his tail, his eyes locked on the other pieces in Sam's hand.

"Just one for now. Don't want you to get fat. Gotta keep you healthy." Sam couldn't bear losing another person. Well, Dooley wasn't a person, but pretty close in his book.

As if understanding, the dog trotted over and nudged Sam's hand with the top of his head, indicating he wanted to be petted. Sam complied. "You liked that walk today, huh?"

"Woof!"

To Sam's surprise, he'd enjoyed it too. He hadn't had much energy or ambition lately, but he was starting to find a little more of it through Dooley—and that silly woman with her newspaper in the car. It had sparked his detective instincts, and for a split second, he'd felt almost... alive.

Sam sighed. Those thoughts were foolish. He was retired and too old for investigating. He had nothing to investigate anyway. All he had was Dooley and waiting around for his sons to visit. Brad lived in California, so that didn't happen often. His other son, Todd, was in Europe, so visits from him happened even less.

He glanced down at the dog, who was looking up at him. "Okay, maybe tomorrow we'll walk a little on the Marginal Way."

"Woof!" Dooley's tail wagged, and he ran to the door.

"Not now. Tomorrow." Sam almost laughed. "Tell you what—we'll go early in the morning."

That appeased Dooley. Early morning was best if Sam wanted to get one of the parking spots, and he didn't mind the chill. Better than the heat, he always said.

The Marginal Way had been one of Jean's favorite walks. They used to walk the entire thing from Perkins Cove to the beach. Sometimes, they would take the trolley back to Perkins Cove if they left the car there. On a good day, they would walk down and back. It was over two miles round trip.

He'd loved walking the winding path with its

gorgeous views of craggy rocks and ocean on one side and lush plantings on the other.

He hadn't been there since the last time with Jean. That time she couldn't even walk anymore, but he'd parked at the little lighthouse and wheeled her along the path. She'd loved it.

He didn't have the energy to walk the whole thing tomorrow. But maybe they could walk a little ways and then sit on one of the benches that looked out at the ocean.

Dooley trotted into the living room, and Sam reached into the cabinet to grab a sandwich bag to store the other pieces of the biscuit in. The cabinets were a bit old, and the countertops were dated. The owl canisters, toaster, and salt and pepper shakers were all where they had been when Jean was still alive. In fact, the whole house was the way it had been, right down to the lighthouse paintings on the wall. He actually never really liked those, but Jean had loved them, and he didn't have the heart to remove them now.

His son had suggested he remodel, but he liked it this way. He was used to it, and why change? If he didn't change anything, then things would stay the same, as if Jean could walk back in at any moment.

There was only one sandwich bag left, but Sam had more in the garage. He always kept backups, because he hated running out. He stored the biscuit pieces in the bag, added sandwich bags to the grocery list, and headed to the garage.

Dooley noticed and rushed over, looking excited. He loved car rides.

"We're not going in the car, buddy." In the garage, Sam glanced across the hood of the white Nissan he normally drove to the car in the second bay. It was covered by a cloth tarp, but he could still picture the candy-apple red of the convertible Corvette underneath. That had been their fun car. They'd loved taking it for rides on weekends.

Sam hadn't taken it out since the last time he'd driven in it with Jean. He hadn't wanted to even look at it, but he'd had his son start it up every few months to make sure it still ran and was in good working order.

He turned away and grabbed the box of sandwich bags.

"Okay, back in the house," he said to Dooley as he held open the door. "No big walk until tomorrow."

Dooley looked excited about the big walk, but the thought made Sam feel exhausted. Maybe tomorrow he'd have more ambition.

CHAPTER SEVEN

*O*arweeds was one of Jane's favorite restaurants. It sat in a little rocky cove on the east side of Perkins Cove, facing the ocean. The beginning of the Marginal Way started right next to the restaurant, and there were small tables set out in between the building and the pathway. It was crowded out there in summer, but this afternoon, it was only Jane, Mike, and Cooper. The weather was cooler, and there weren't many tourists, which suited Jane just fine. They wouldn't have been able to bring Cooper with them if they ate inside, so she simply snuggled into a thick cable-knit sweater and enjoyed the cozy feeling.

"How was the book club meeting?" Mike dipped a steamed clam into broth and then butter. They'd decided to start off with steamers, and then both had ordered salads with lobster on top for their meals.

"It was fun. I never realized there were so many things to discuss about a book." Jane had enjoyed reading the murder mystery and was excited about the next book they'd chosen. "Bunny Howard was really into deciphering all the clues."

Mike laughed. "That sounds like her."

"She even got suspicious of our one guest." Mike had been disappointed that they even had a guest, though he hadn't made a big deal out of it. Jane would have been able to spend more time with him if she didn't have anything to attend to at Tides. That was why she'd hired Liz, but Liz hadn't been there very long, so Jane was still a little reluctant to be away for too long.

"Why? What did he do?" Mike pulled another clam out of the shell, and Cooper looked up at him expectantly. "I don't think you like clams, buddy."

"He knew we were having snacks, and I guess he came down looking for them and got lost."

"Lost? The place isn't that big."

"We were in the sitting room way in the back, and somehow, he ended up down there. Bunny thought he was lurking and listening."

Mike's left brow quirked up. "Oh. Is that the room you said your dad always wanted to make into a library?"

"Yes. That's why I thought it would be perfect for the book club." Fleeting memories of the plans she and her dad had made for the room bubbled up—where to place bookcases, what kinds of furniture. Jane always regretted not following through on those. Maybe someday. For now, she would just be happy they were putting the room to use for the book club.

"He was probably just unsure if he should barge in to get a snack."

"Well, the food was actually in the dining room." Jane pulled a roll out of the basket. It was still warm.

"Oh, then I guess that is weird. Wouldn't he have had to walk past it to get to the room you were in?"

"Sure, but he probably didn't even see the food in there. He heard our voices and followed them."

"I see. Still seems weird. And it is odd that he was in the hardware store. I hope he's not some creeper. I want you to be safe at Tides."

"Cooper will protect me." Jane wasn't worried. She looked down at the dog, who smiled up at her as if agreeing that he would protect her. Then something Mike had said hit her. *How did he know Mr. Smith was in the hardware store?* "You saw him in the hardware store? Were you with Andie?"

Andie had said she'd seen Mr. Smith there too. And didn't Liz say Andie was with Mike at the inn? Seemed like a lot of coincidences.

"Andie? No. I wasn't with her." Mike focused on buttering a roll.

51

"Oh, I think she mentioned seeing Smith downtown too."

"Lots of people go there. Why would Andie be in the hardware store? If you need something fixed, I can do it."

"She didn't mention why she was there. Why do you think Mr. Smith would be in there?"

"Maybe Andie has him fixing something at Tides," Mike joked.

The waitress brought their meals, and they concentrated on digging in. The lobster was buttery and sweet; the salad was crisp.

"So, I was hoping now that you have Liz to cover and since it's the slow time for the inn that you could stay over more," Mike said. "I cleaned out a space in my closet."

Jane looked up, her heart melting at the hopeful sparkle in Mike's green eyes. He'd been asking her to stay over more and more… even mentioned something more "permanent," whatever that meant. Jane loved Mike, but she wasn't sure she was ready. Her first husband had died not long after they were married, and she still had some unresolved issues around that.

But she didn't want to disappoint Mike. "Liz is doing well, so I guess I could stay over more."

Cooper gave a soft woof and wagged his tail.

"Cooper is excited about that," Mike said.

Jane was excited, too, but she couldn't push away

the nagging feeling that Mike was leaving something out about being with Andie and how her mother had mentioned him.

"Did you visit Mom at Tall Pines yesterday? She mentioned seeing Cooper and something about measuring."

"No. I … Oops." Mike dropped his roll, and Cooper scarfed it up. "Guess you got an extra treat."

Jane's brow furrowed. Was he avoiding her question?

He sipped his water. "I mean, yes, I was there. You know how I take Cooper once a week. Brightens people's day. And, of course, I dropped in on Addie. I don't know what she means about measuring, though."

That made sense. Jane was probably making too much of her mother's remark. With her dementia, she often said things that weren't reality. "Probably one of her confusions."

"Probably. But she seemed good overall," Mike said.

Jane smiled and dug into her lobster salad, certain she was making too much of everything. Bunny's suspicions and the mystery books they were reading must have put her in a suspicious mode. Everything was perfectly fine, wasn't it?

*J*ane stopped in at Bradford Breads on the way back from her lunch with Mike. The bread store was set up like something between a bakery and a country store. Loaves of fresh bread sat in display cases and on wooden racks. Strategically placed old barrel-shaped tables held spreads, honey, jams, and other things one might put on bread. The homey smell of sourdough permeated the air and made Jane's mouth water even though she'd just come from lunch.

"Hey, Jane!" Claire came out of the back, with Rob just behind her. Their cheeks were flushed, and Jane's brows rose automatically. Rob was a nice guy and handsome, too, with his dark silver-tinged hair and deephazel eyes. She was glad that he and Claire had developed a relationship. She was about to make a joke about them baking in back when Claire's gaze skidded past her to the window.

"Is that Cooper in the car?"

Jane turned. Since she was just running in, she'd left him sitting in the passenger seat with the windows cracked open. "Yep. We just came from a late lunch with Mike."

"Perfect, because I happen to have some dog biscuits for him in my purse. I was going to drop them off at Tides." Claire darted into the back again and returned a few seconds later with a bakery bag in her hand.

"Thanks. Cooper loves these," Jane said. "How are sales going for them?"

"Really good. I've been thinking about brand names, though I guess I might have some work to do on that."

"Oh, really? Why do you need a brand name?" Jane asked.

Claire shrugged. "I don't really, but maybe if I wanted to package them and sell them online or something. Unlike my pastries, they stay good for a while and could easily be shipped. I came up with a good name, but there might be a glitch."

Rob had gone over to one of the racks to grab her loaves of bread, and he returned, handing them to Jane before slipping behind the counter to the cash register.

"What's the glitch?" Jane fumbled in her purse for her card to pay Rob.

Claire sighed. "Well, I came up with the name Beach Bones, and I've had a few customers say that someone else is already using it."

"Oh, and you have your mind set that it's the name you want to use?" Jane asked.

Claire made a face. "Sort of."

"You know how she is when she has her mind made up." Rob smiled at Claire fondly. "But even if someone else is using it, you can too. Just make sure it's not trade-marked or anything."

"I have Tammi looking into that."

"Well, sounds like it should work itself out easily then. I'll keep my fingers crossed for you." Jane took her card back from Rob and left with her packages of bread and the dog biscuits.

She hesitated at the car, juggling everything she was carrying as she unlocked it. Her eyes drifted to the hardware store. She couldn't help but think it was odd that both Mike and Andie had mentioned Smith in the hardware store. Not to mention she wondered what the guy was doing in there. Of course, it could have been a dozen things. Maybe he was picking something up for back home or needed some thumbtacks or to have a key made. *Hopefully not the one for his room.* Jane shook her head. Now she was starting to think like Bunny!

Of course, both Mike and Andie had dozens of reasons to be downtown too. Neither of them had been in the store. They'd just seen Mr. Smith… which meant they had been there at pretty much the same time. But that wasn't so odd, was it? Her gaze drifted over the stores in view of the hardware store: the candy store, the frame store, the trinket store, the jewelry store—

Wait a minute… jewelry store. Her heart hitched. A few weeks ago, Mike had mentioned something to the effect of making their relationship more permanent. Liz had thought Andie and Mike were at Tides together. Addie had said Mike was asking about sizes and measurements. Could they all be conspiring over an engagement ring?

CHAPTER EIGHT

*E*arly the next morning, Bunny plunged her hand into the little tide pool beside the rock on the beach. The water was freezing! She pulled out her hand, clutching the moon snail shell. No snail was inside, and it was perfect for her to use to capture the exact subtle colors of lavender and gray in her painting.

She dropped it into her tote bag and turned to face the ocean. The sun had come up an hour ago and it warmed her face. Taking a deep breath, she basked in the beauty of the ocean, the salty air, the sound of the waves, and the serenity of being the only one on the small beach.

Bunny loved this time of year. The cool air was refreshing, there were hardly any tourists, and the beaches were so peaceful. Especially the small ones along the Marginal Way, like the one she was on now.

These beaches were sparsely populated even in summer, because they were covered with water when the tide came in.

There was something exciting about being the only one in sight, standing with the vast ocean in front of you—except, she wasn't the *only* one there. A man was walking along the outcropping of rocks that formed a cliff a little ways down. It was a good spot; she'd walked there many times herself. From there, the wide river to the beach was visible. It was slippery up there, though. At high tide, the ocean splashed up over the rocks. She'd found starfish, sea urchins, and crabs up there. There was always a covering of slippery seaweed clinging to the rocks, and she'd fallen a few times.

She hoped the man didn't fall. *Hmm…* He looked kind of familiar.

Bunny shaded her eyes and squinted to see better. *Wait! Is that Mr. Smith? And what does he have in his hand?* Something big and round.

She watched as he picked his way across the rocks. He stopped at the edge, looked over, then raised the round thing level with his shoulders before letting it drop.

Bunny gasped as it smashed on the jagged rocks below.

What in the world?

She watched as Mr. Smith then leaned over the side. He pulled something out of his pocket. A rope? A string? He slid it over the side, letting it down almost to the bottom.

Is he measuring?

A chill ran down Bunny's spine. In the mystery book, the killer had counted the number of stairs it would take for the victim to become seriously hurt in much the same manner.

Was Mr. Smith plotting to push someone off the cliff? It wasn't a tall cliff, only about twenty or thirty feet, but the rocks below would do a lot of damage. Just ask the cantaloupe that was now smashed to pieces on them.

Mr. Smith walked back to the path and disappeared.

Bunny scrambled up the stairs to the path and headed in that direction to see exactly what Mr. Smith had been up to.

*S*am had walked farther than he'd intended, but Dooley had wanted to keep going. Sam was surprised to discover that he didn't mind. They'd walked up to where the path had a little shortcut through a wooded area. In this little area was a series of copper plaques with the names of people who had donated to the upkeep of the path.

Sam's eyes misted as he read through the names. At the bottom were empty spaces for more names.

Jean's name was on the list to be printed on one of those.

As if sensing his sadness, Dooley pressed against Sam's leg and snuffed his hand.

That brought a smile to Sam's face. And when he looked up at the ocean to see the sun kissing the tops of the waves, heard the birds chirping in the trees, and felt the sea breeze on his face, his heart lifted. Maybe there were still things to be grateful for.

"Let's go back to the car, eh?"

Dooley looked a little disappointed.

"Okay, maybe we'll sit on one of the benches for a spell."

Dooley's tail wagged in response.

Sam felt a little lighter as they walked back. He chose a bench not far from the car, overlooking the little beaches that were revealed when the tide receded. Maybe tomorrow, he'd take Dooley down onto the beach. He knew the dog would like that.

He took out a treat and fed it to Dooley, who had settled in at his feet. When Dooley didn't take the treat right away, Sam looked down to see Dooley was busy staring at something to the left.

Sam followed his gaze to see a person scurrying over the rocks at the base of the cliff.

What in the world? Wait a minute... The silver-tinted auburn hair looked familiar. *Is that the woman from the car? And what in the world is she doing?*

It looked like she was inspecting something on the rocks. She held up a piece of something that looked like a cantaloupe rind. How odd.

Then she rummaged in her tote, pulling out a variety of things before settling on a... *What is that? A measuring tape?*

He felt a pang of something in his gut, something he hadn't felt in a long time. It was his detective instincts. The instincts that had allowed him to catch hundreds of criminals. The instincts that had given him a purpose in life. The instincts that he thought were long gone.

He leaned forward, feeling that spark of excitement he used to get. His days on the force were long over, but this woman and her odd behavior made him wonder if maybe he didn't necessarily need to be on official police business to investigate. She was clearly up to something, and maybe he could find out what it was. Of course, if it was something criminal, then he would report his findings to the police. He still had contacts.

But there was something about the woman that made him hope she wasn't some kind of criminal. Maybe it was her auburn hair, which reminded him of Jean's hair, or maybe it was the air of determination that radiated from her.

He noticed how she was gingerly stepping over the rocks. He guessed her to be around his age, but she didn't seem to be afraid of falling and breaking something. Nope, she had a clear purpose and wasn't going to let anything stop her. She was clearly not a useless old person.

Was that what he'd become? Jean wouldn't like that at all. And with that thought, he felt something shift inside him. It was as if Jean were reaching out to give him a nudge.

Here was something he could do to get back into the swing of things and make himself feel useful again.

He had a million ideas on how to find out who the woman was and what she was up to. He found himself hoping she wasn't up to anything too nefarious. He was also hoping she didn't fall. Despite her suspicious behavior, there was something he liked about her.

"Woof!"

"You think so too?" He fed Dooley a treat. "We're almost out of these. Better make a trip to Sandcastles to get some more. I think we've just found ourselves something interesting to do."

CHAPTER NINE

"I'll have a half moon and two cannoli please."

Claire turned from wiping down the coffee station to see Bunny Howard standing at the bakery case. Her face was flushed, and she looked excited. "Hi, Bunny. How are you?"

"Great. You? Have you started the new book yet?"

Claire grabbed a pastry tissue and reached into the case for the half-vanilla-half-chocolate frosted pastries. "Not yet, but I'm looking forward to our new book club meeting."

"Me too. I think I have the killer worked out in this book too." Bunny leaned closer, which wasn't easy to do since she was not much taller than the case. "I think I'm getting pretty good at working out mysteries."

Claire slid the pastries into the bag and opened the

other side of the case for the cannoli. "You did a good job on the last book."

"Yes. And it's not just in books, either." Bunny glanced around and lowered her voice. "But I'll keep mum until I have real evidence."

"Evidence?" Bunny certainly was overly dramatic this morning.

Bunny waved her hand in the air. "Don't mind me! Just silly chatter."

Claire's eyes narrowed. She didn't take Bunny for a silly chatterer, but she could tell that she wasn't going to get any more out of her. The book club mysteries certainly were having an influence on her, but she appeared to be having fun, so what was the harm?

She rang up Bunny's purchase and watched her leave.

Sam was outside, tying Dooley up at the post by the door. His eyes followed Bunny as she got into her pale-blue car.

Did Sam seem a little less stooped today? That was good. Dooley was having a good effect on him. He still had a sad air about him, but if she wasn't mistaken, she'd seen a teeny bit of spark in his eyes as he walked in the door. Did that have something to do with Bunny?

"How are you, Sam?"

"Great. Just took Dooley for a walk on the Marginal Way. Haven't been there in a while."

66

Maybe that was what was responsible for Sam's apparent vigor and it had nothing to do with Bunny.

He turned to face the door. "Say, isn't that the woman who... Um... Oh, what is her name? The one in the blue car."

Claire leaned over to see out the window. "You mean Bunny."

Claire understood Sam's forgetfulness. It happened to her more often than she liked to admit, and Sam had a few decades on her.

Sam snapped his fingers. "Yes, that's it! Bunny Johnson."

"Bunny Howard."

"Oh, right." Sam looked sheepish. "Memory isn't all that. I remember her from a while back. Guess I should have said hi."

"I'm sure you'll have plenty of chances to see her again. She comes in quite regularly."

"She does, does she?" Sam shuffled over to the section where the dog biscuits were, and Claire followed.

"Yep, and she's part of our new book club at Tides." Claire looked over the case at him. "You might want to join that."

Sam frowned as if considering it. "Oh, I don't know. Maybe." His demeanor seemed to dim, and Claire wished she hadn't said anything.

"How many?" Claire held up the dog biscuit bag.

"I'll take four." Sam smiled as if to offset his rejection of the book club.

A woman was perusing the items in the case. She pointed at the biscuits as Claire took out four for Sam.

"Oh, you carry Beach Bones. My dog loves those. I got some down in Wells," the woman said.

"Wells? I only sell them here. These are my own recipe," Claire said proudly. The woman was probably confused about some other dog biscuits, but Claire hoped she'd try hers.

"Oh. Well, the others were named something similar. I thought it was a brand from a big store. My mistake. I'll try some of yours, though."

Claire was happy to sell the woman some Beach Bones, but now she was feeling little uneasy, especially since she remembered someone mentioning they'd seen that name the other day. Maybe changing her name was best, but Claire was getting sort of attached to the name. And besides, if someone had copied her, then she didn't want them to think they could just take her name for the biscuits. She made a mental note to have Tammi step up the pace on her trademark research.

*S*am untied Dooley and gave him half a treat.

"I still got it, boy." Sam chuckled. "Did you see how I got Claire to tell me the name of that woman?"

Dooley looked up at him, and Sam imagined he was nodding his agreement.

Sam had used an old trick he'd employed as a detective. When he was on the force and wanted to know someone's identity, he would pretend he'd forgotten their name. It worked every time. Of course, a bakery in a small seaside town was a bit easier than in the city, but it accomplished the same thing. It probably worked even better now that he was older. People seemed to just assume folks his age were forgetful, even though his memory was as sharp as ever.

A pang of guilt bubbled up over tricking Claire. It felt a bit like lying, and Sam didn't like that, but it was for a good cause. He liked Claire, and it had warmed his heart that she'd invited him to the book club. He wouldn't join it, of course. He preferred sitting at home and... and what? Watching television with Dooley? Doing crossword puzzles? Maybe he should consider joining. He did love to read.

But the thought of getting out there and socializing without Jean made a heavy pit form in his stomach. Maybe he'd consider it later on. For now, he had some work to do. He needed to figure out where Bunny

Howard lived so he could set up a little surveillance. Not like a stalker or anything, more like what he used to do back in his police days. He still knew how to follow someone without being noticed. At least he thought he still did.

Sam picked up the pace to his car. He couldn't wait to get home. For once, he had something to look forward to.

CHAPTER TEN

*J*ane practically ran Maxi over on her way to double check that they'd cleaned up all the crumbs and polished off the coffee mug rings from their book club meeting the other night.

"Oh! Sorry!" Maxi had a sketchbook open in her hand and was busy drawing in it, which wasn't that unusual. What was unusual was that she was standing in the middle of the hallway while doing it.

"What are you drawing?" Jane craned her neck to peek into the book, and Maxi snapped it shut.

"I was just putting the finishing touches on a drawing. You know how I get lost in them."

"Standing in the hall?"

"I started outside."

Andie came down the hallway. "What's going on?"

"Oh, nothing. We just bumped into each other," Maxi said.

"I was on my way to the back room to make sure we'd cleaned everything up after the book club meeting," Jane said, wondering why she suddenly felt like she had to explain herself.

Andie held up a cleaning cloth in one hand and some crumpled napkins and a bookmark in another. "No need. I just cleaned it. But I do have something to talk to you about. Let's go to the kitchen."

Andie breezed toward the kitchen, and Jane turned and followed with Maxi behind her.

When they passed the foyer, Maxi headed for the door. "I gotta get back to my cottage and finish this up." She tapped on the sketch pad. "See you guys later."

"Why was she sketching from here? She has her own cottage on the beach," Jane said as she and Andie continued to the kitchen.

"Different vantage point. From here, you can see part of the Marginal Way. Can't see that from her cottage." Andie turned to look at her. "You're awfully suspicious. I think those mystery books are getting to you."

Andie might have a point. Maxi had painted from their deck before, so it wasn't exactly unusual.

Liz was in the kitchen with a trash bag open in front of her. She looked startled when she heard them come in. "Oh, hi. I emptied the trash from the rooms. Well, our one room."

Emptied? To Jane, it looked like she was going through the trash, not emptying it. But maybe she was being too suspicious, as Andie had just pointed out.

"Perfect. I have some trash to throw in from the book club meeting." Andie shoved the trash in her hand into the bag, and Liz tied up the bag and headed to the kitchen door to the small dumpster that sat just outside.

"I'll just toss this out and then head home, unless you guys need something else?"

"No, we're good. See you in a few days." Andie opened the door for Liz and then turned to Jane. "I'm glad I caught you. I have a proposition."

"You do?"

"Yes, I was hoping you could come to the New England Antique Inns and Furnishings Conference with me in a couple of days. It's in Bar Harbor."

"Umm… okay. What is it?" Jane was caught a little off-guard. She'd never heard of the conference and didn't do well with quick decisions.

"It's an industry conference for owners of antique inns. I found out about it in the *Antique Digest* newsletter I get for my shop. It could be a great way to make some contacts with advertisers that have leads for people that like to stay at old inns, and we can see some of the furniture that will fit in with our antiques."

Jane looked around. She liked all their antiques but

had to admit that sometimes they weren't all that practical. "It would be nice to have a more useful place to serve coffee other than having it drip all over Great-grandma Miller's bird's-eye maple server."

"And maybe see if they have any antique-style beverage coolers," Andie said. "Plus, there could be tons of magazines we should be advertising in but just don't know about."

"That does sound like a good idea." In the spring, when Jane had taken over running the inn because of their mother's memory problems, she had been worried about getting enough guests. Her mother had let things go, and they'd lost a lot of their repeat business. But now things were picking up. Still, it did make good business sense to see if she could make some contacts that would allow her to expand her advertising.

"Liz said she'd keep an eye on things, and with only one guest, I don't think anyone really needs to be in attendance here, do you? Maybe we could stay overnight. We could go out to a nice restaurant and spend some sister time." Andie looked overly hopeful.

"Now you're talking," Jane said. "Do you really think we could leave the inn overnight?"

"I've already talked to Liz, and she'll be happy to stay in one of the rooms, but I also think we don't need to be here at night as long as no guests are checking in. Our one guest will be fine here all alone. And Brenda still comes every morning."

"True. Okay, overnight it is." Jane didn't want to miss a chance to spend time with Andie. The two hadn't been very close most of their adult lives and had just recently reconnected. Jane didn't want to waste one minute of that.

It would be a good test of her resolve to spend less time at the inn. Mike would surely like that. But now worry about what Mike was up to snuck into her thoughts. Liz had thought Andie was with Mike this morning, and they'd both seemed a bit cagey about seeing Mr. Smith at the hardware store. Was Andie in on Mike's plan? If so, the trip might be a good opportunity to try to wheedle it out of her. And maybe she should even ask Andie for advice, because if Mike really was planning to propose, what would her answer be?

"Great!" Andie said. "I gotta get to the antiques shop. We're still meeting at Splash tonight for dinner, right?"

Jane glanced outside. She, Andie, Maxi, and Claire, along with their significant others, usually dined out together a couple of times a month. "It's still warm enough, so I think so."

"Great, see you tonight!"

CHAPTER ELEVEN

*B*unny mixed some warm gray with just a touch of king's blue light paint and dabbed it onto the canvas right at the apex of the moon snail shell. Most people thought the shells were rather plain, but Bunny wasn't most people. She saw the beauty in the shell, especially when under water and the intricate blue, gray, and purple colors became more vibrant.

Of all the snail shells on the beach, the moon snails were one of her favorites. The snail itself could live for fifteen years—most people didn't know that. And it was one of the few that ate other snails. Their unique characteristics aside, Bunny just liked to paint them.

Glancing at the shell she'd picked up off the beach for reference, she blended the colors. Her thoughts drifted to that morning on the beach and the nefarious activity she'd seen Mr. Smith engaging in.

After he left, she'd checked out the smashed cantaloupe lying on the rocks. It was a bit disturbing, like a smashed skull. It made her wonder, though, if pushing someone off the cliff could cause a deadly accident. Maybe Mr. Smith was wondering the same thing.

She still hadn't come up with a plan of action for further investigation. Should she just lurk outside of Tides and wait for him to go somewhere? That seemed a bit inefficient. She didn't want anyone to see her and think she was up to something... Though now that she thought about it, she had seen that cute hound dog that had been around her car when she'd been surveilling Smith more than once in the past few days. And if she had seen him more than once, than maybe his owner had seen her. She needed to be a bit more discreet.

A knock on the slider startled her out of her thoughts. Liz was outside, having used the path between their gardens as usual. She looked anxious. Maybe she had intel on Mr. Smith.

Bunny set her paints aside and rushed to let Liz in.

"I'm not interrupting your painting, am I?" Liz glanced at the canvas.

Bunny waved her hand. "Not at all. I can paint any time. Come in the kitchen. Coffee? Tea?"

"Tea would be great." Liz followed her into the kitchen.

Bunny put on some water and put the little basket with a variety of tea bags on the table. She grabbed two mugs and sat, putting one in front of Liz, who had a paper on the table in front of her.

"What's that?" Bunny tilted her head to see what it was. The paper looked crumpled and stained with handwriting in black pen.

Liz grimaced. "Well, I probably shouldn't have taken this, but I was emptying the trash, and it sort of stuck out. It came from Mr. Smith's room. Aren't these all poisons?"

She shoved the paper in front of Bunny. On it were four words, one on top of the other: *hemlock*, *nightshade*, *death cap*, and *dapperling*.

"These are poisons. Natural ones that can be found in the woods." *Poison?* That was strange. Judging by his behavior on the beach, Bunny had assumed Mr. Smith was thinking about pushing someone off the cliff. Perhaps this was a backup plan. But she didn't want to say that to Liz, because Liz looked worried.

"You don't think he plans to poison someone, do you?" Liz asked.

The tea kettle whistled, and Bunny poured the water into their mugs. "Don't worry, dear. I highly doubt he's planning to poison people at random. Besides, that list could be for anything. Those last two are mushrooms. Perhaps he's going mushroom collecting and wants to make sure to avoid poison mushrooms and herbs. Isn't fall good for mushrooms?" Bunny actually thought the warm summer weather was better for mushrooms, but her statement seemed to quell Liz's fears.

"Oh, that could be! I heard him making plans to meet someone at the Rachel Carson Refuge. They probably have tons of mushrooms there."

"You did?" The Rachel Carson National Wildlife Refuge was one of Bunny's favorite places. Named after the late marine biologist who'd dedicated her life to wildlife conservation, it consisted of over nine thousand acres of forest, coastal meadows, and salt marshes. "I love to go see the deer in the fields there."

"Me too. Dad used to take us when we were kids." Liz smiled at the memory. "I guess that's what Mr. Smith must be doing, too, because he did say he would meet the person around dusk tonight."

"See then? Nothing suspicious about this at all." Bunny tapped the paper, smiled, and sipped her tea, all the while thinking that dusk was the perfect time for a murder and the Rachel Carson Refuge was a great place to hide a body.

"Right. I guess it was silly of me," Liz said.

"Not at all! I'm glad you brought it over. He did act suspicious the night of the book club, but that was probably my imagination. Now, would you like some carrot cake to go with the tea?"

Bunny made a mental inventory as she cut the cake. *Binoculars, vest with pockets, camera.* Now all she had to do was go to the refuge a little bit before dusk, and she could easily get into place so that she could follow Mr. Smith and prevent him from doing whatever horrible thing he intended to do.

t didn't take much effort for Sam to discover who Bunny Howard was and where she lived. She seemed like a normal person. She liked painting, was a widow, and had lived in her house for forty years. She was about Sam's age, but of course, he already knew that.

"It's kind of scary all this information is right out on the internet," Sam said to Dooley. They were sitting in his kitchen, the late afternoon sun slanting in through the window.

The old owl canisters that had sat on the counter for decades were now upside down on the drying rack. Sam had thrown out the old sugar and flour that had been inside them. He wasn't sure what he'd do with them, maybe get new ones. It might be time for some changes.

"Don't worry. Not too many changes," Sam said out loud just in case Dooley knew what he was thinking. It sure seemed like the dog did sometimes.

Sam should have been tired. He'd had more activity in the past few days than he'd had in two years, but he felt energized. After looking up information on Bunny, he'd driven past her house, feeling a little bit like a creeper. He'd convinced himself he was only a guy taking his dog out for a ride. It felt good to get out of the house.

The neighborhood was nice, full of mature landscaping and well-kept lawns. The homes were neatly painted and trimmed, with enough space for privacy but not too much. He felt like people could be neighborly there. He'd known his neighbors when Jean was alive, but most of them had moved in the last few years. And since Jean's death, he'd stayed in his house like a hermit, not venturing out to meet the new ones, even though they all seemed friendly and waved to him whenever they saw him out in the yard.

Bunny's car had been in the driveway of her modest ranch house. As Sam had driven past, a woman had come out of the side door. In his detective days, that would have raised his suspicions, but this was a suburban neighborhood, and neighbors often used back doors. Jean had done so herself many times when the Crosbys had lived next door to them.

He hadn't been able to learn much else about Bunny Howard. She certainly didn't seem like a suspicious character, but in his experience, those could be the worst kind.

But what to do next? Perhaps he should just forget about the strange things he'd seen her doing. It wasn't like he was a detective acting in any official capacity. On the other hand, what else did he have to do?

Dooley trotted over to his leash, which Sam kept hanging from the doorknob. "Woof!"

"You want to go for a ride?"

"Woof!"

It was a nice evening for a ride. And if he happened to drive through Bunny's neighborhood, then who would notice?

His car was in the garage, and he led Dooley out then opened the passenger side for the dog to hop in. As he turned, he brushed against the cloth tarp covering the Corvette, revealing a glimpse of the cherry-red paint underneath. A spark of excitement bubbled up.

What would it feel like to drive the Vette again? But that car would be much too conspicuous for following someone. He'd be spotted right away. And besides, those days were long gone, and he should probably think about selling it.

Sam brushed away the thought. He didn't need the money, and there was plenty of time to think about that later. Right now, he had more important things to do. He had a suspect to follow.

CHAPTER TWELVE

*S*plash was one of Jane and her friends' favorite restaurants to gather at because it was situated directly on the beach. In fact, they liked it so much that over the summer, the four couples had gotten into the habit of eating there a couple of nights each month. The restaurant officially closed just after Labor Day, but the owner opened it on select nights when the weather was warm enough, and tonight was one of those nights.

The restaurant wasn't anything fancy, but its patio just above the sugar-soft sand offered an unobstructed view of the ocean that couldn't be beat.

The sun set behind them to the West, but the colors on the ocean were always fantastic. And it was always a treat to smell the salty sea air and listen to the soothing sound of the waves. Even the seagulls that hopped along outside the patio waiting for a morsel of food were fun to watch.

It was warm for October, but Jane had worn her thickest sweater coat. Maxi must've been feeling the chill; she even had fingerless gloves on. Claire, on the other hand, was wearing only a light jacket. Perhaps she was suffering from hot flashes. Jane had heard her complain about them a few times.

Andie and her boyfriend, Shane, had arrived a little late. They'd decided to eat around four in the afternoon to take advantage of the afternoon warmth and be finished by the time it got darker and cooler. Shane had had to rush from his renovation job. He'd apologized for not changing first, but with his tall, muscular body and close-cropped salt-and-pepper hair, he could easily pull off a flannel shirt and jeans with a bit of sawdust still clinging to them and look like he'd dressed that way on purpose.

Everyone had assured him there was no need to apologize as they sat back with their drinks and plastic cups that had colorful stirrers in the shapes of crabs, starfish, and mermaids sticking out of them.

"It's getting chilly. I suppose this will be our last dinner out here until next summer." Rob's voice held a tinge of regret.

"Maybe after this, we can move the dinners inside to Tides for the winter. There's plenty of room for all eight of us in the dining room," Jane said.

"Will you still be living at Tides then?" Claire wiggled her eyebrows and glanced from Mike to Jane.

She should talk—she'd been dating Rob much longer, and the two of them still had separate places. But her reaction made Jane wonder if there really was something going on behind her back. First Mike and Andie seeming to be in the same places and not telling her, and now this little comment.

She glanced at Mike, but he didn't seem at all concerned and was happily taking a swig of beer.

"I think I will still be living there. But it doesn't really matter. We can still use Tides. I don't have to be living in the inn for us to use the dining room. In fact, now that we have Liz to help out, I'm not needed there as much. And no one actually needs to stay overnight. All the guests have keys to the front door." Come to think of it, it wouldn't be so bad if Jane did get another place. The owner's suite in Tides was kind of small and consisted of just a bedroom and sitting area. Then again, it was nice to be on location in case something happened and she was needed.

"Jane and I are going away to Bar Harbor overnight," Andie chimed in.

"You are?" Maxi looked excited. "I went up there to get some inspiration for a painting a couple of weeks ago. It's beautiful there."

Andie nodded. "There's an antique hotels conference there, and Jane and I are going to catch the conference and then spend some sister time."

Andie leaned over and put an arm around Jane's shoulder. It warmed Jane's heart, but had Andie's gaze flicked to Mike for a split second? Mike didn't seem to acknowledge anything, though. Maybe it was Jane's imagination.

"You're leaving the inn all alone with the mysterious Mr. Smith?" Rob asked as he passed around the basket of bread the waitress had left on the table.

"Have you been talking to Bunny?" Jane laughed.

"She was in Sandcastles this morning, talking about evidence." Claire slid the butter over to James, Maxi's husband.

James frowned. "What kind of evidence?"

"She wouldn't say. If you ask me, that woman has too much time on her hands," Claire said.

"And reads too many mysteries," Andie added.

"But you have to admit, Mr. Smith is a little mysterious." Jane picked out a roll. It was still warm, and steam wafted out when she pulled it open.

"What does he do? Do you even know why he's in town?" Maxi asked.

Jane shrugged. "No idea. But people have lots of reasons for coming to town, and we try not to pry."

"That's smart," Claire said.

"Anyway, what's going on at the bakery? How are your dog biscuits doing?" Jane automatically reached down to pet Cooper, who was sitting beside her on the patio. His tail wagged excitedly as soon as she mentioned dog biscuits.

Instead of looking excited, Claire's brow creased into a frown. "Well, people seem to like them, but I think there might be someone else using the same name. I've had Tammi research it, and she says nothing is trademarked or anything, so I guess I can use it…"

"You sound uncertain about that." James, Maxi's husband, was a banker and knew a bit about legal things. "If no one else has trademarked it, you have every right."

"I know. But it feels a little strange. I wish I knew who was using it or even if someone really is. Some of my customers seem a little uncertain about the exact name." Claire shrugged and took a sip of her drink. "But I really like the name, and if someone is copying *me*, then I'm certainly not going to be the one to stop using it."

"Yeah, don't let someone else make you change your plan," Andie said.

"I won't. What about you? Any great finds at the antique store?" Claire asked.

Andie had once worked for Christie's auction house in New York City, dealing with high-end antiques and hoping to make an important antique discovery. But when their mom had gotten sick, Andie had come back to help out. And Jane was grateful that she'd fallen back in love with their small town and real-ized she could have a fulfilling career right here in Lobster Bay.

She hadn't made any big discoveries, but she'd helped the people, and that was more important. Of course, reuniting with her high school boyfriend, Shane, might have had something to do with her decision to stay, but Jane liked to think that being close to family was the main reason.

"No great finds this week," Andie joked. "It's actu-ally kind of slow. Do you guys know the house out on Ledge Road that's been boarded up for years?"

Jane knew the house well. It was a big old Victorian with chipped paint, shutters hanging on their hinges, and spindles missing on the porch. "If I recall, there was some sort of mystery surrounding that house, wasn't there?" Jane asked.

Andy nodded. "Yeah. Something about a missing woman. I'm not really sure exactly, anyway, but a woman came in saying that she owns it and she's moving out here from Ohio. Apparently, it's full of stuff, and she was wondering if I would look at some of it."

Jane could sense Andie's excitement. There was nothing her sister loved more than old houses full of stuff.

"Really?" Rob asked. "I thought that house had been boarded up for decades. You mean no one has gotten in there to ruin it yet?"

"I guess not. Maybe the rumor about it being haunted has kept people away."

Everyone laughed at Andie's joke. When they were kids, someone had still lived there, even though Jane seemed to recall it was quite dilapidated even back then.

The waitress came by, and they all ordered. Jane chose her usual lobster roll. She liked the way they made it with little bits of celery on a toasted hotdog bun.

As they waited for the meal, they settled into the familiar banter of old friends, catching up on town happenings and what each of them had done during the week.

"I noticed you put a place up for people to tie their dogs outside Sandcastles. Do you have anything for cats?" James joked. Maxi and James had two kittens, Rembrandt and Picasso, that they adored.

"If you think your cats will stay tied up to a post, you're welcome to bring them." Claire laughed. "But people seem to really appreciate it. Everyone got used to bringing their dogs with them to sit out on the patio this summer, but now that it's been too cold to sit out most of the time, at least they can have them right outside."

"I noticed Sam Campbell's dog out there. It's good to see them getting out," Maxi said.

Claire smiled. "Isn't it? He's been in such a funk after Jean's passing. Barely even left the house, from what I hear. Hardly saw him at the bakery, but he's been in a few times this week, and his spirits seem to be picking up. He was even asking about Bunny Howard."

"He was? Maybe it is a little romance there." Andie wiggled her eyebrows.

"I think they'd make a cute couple. Maybe that will take Bunny's mind off Mr. Smith. She does seem a little obsessed with proving that he is up to something," Claire said.

"Liz said that Bunny has been talking about him too. Poor Mr. Smith. He's probably just a regular guy that only wants some peace and quiet. I do hope she doesn't do anything drastic that could get her into trouble."

CHAPTER THIRTEEN

*B*unny wasn't going to do anything drastic that would get her into trouble. She was simply going to observe. Of course, she might have to intervene if Mr. Smith tried any funny business on his companion. What she would do to intervene, she had no idea. Perhaps she would be able to detain him and call 911. Though Mr. Smith was a bit younger, taller, and stronger than her, she wasn't afraid.

She'd arrived well ahead of dusk and parked in an inconspicuous spot down the road. She then headed into the woods to wait for Mr. Smith's arrival. She didn't mind waiting. While she was there, she would take advantage of the beautiful scenery. The leaves were starting to turn, and there were splashes of bright orange, yellow, and scarlet mixed in with the lush green on the trees.

The refuge was filled with trails, and she was happy to explore them, taking pictures of the colorful flowers and fall foliage for her painting endeavors as she waited for Mr. Smith to show up.

She was careful to always stay within sight of the parking lot so she could be alerted when Mr. Smith's car came in, and it did about an hour later. Soon, another car pulled up behind him. That looked like a clandestine meeting if she'd ever seen one.

She watched as the two men disappeared down the trail. They seemed to be talking amicably. Perhaps Mr. Smith was lulling his victim into complacency.

Bunny was quite familiar with all the trails and where they led, so she was able to follow Mr. Smith on a parallel trail without being seen. After a few minutes, she saw them come to a small clearing and sit on a bench that overlooked a marshy area. To her disappointment, they simply continued talking.

Bunny considered her options. She could wait for Mr. Smith to make his move and then intervene, or she could try to warn his companion. The latter option seemed the safest, but if she did that, she wouldn't be able to get any evidence, and Mr. Smith might just deny he was up to something.

She wished she could overhear what they were talking about. Perhaps she should creep closer. But the sun was setting, and the light was fading. Everything was turning to a gloomy stone-gray color.

She could take the southeastern path and come around behind them. The forest was a little denser over there, and it was getting darker. Perhaps this really was just an innocent meeting between Mr. Smith and his companion.

But wait a minute! What was that flash in the woods? It looked like the sun glinting off the lenses of a pair of binoculars.

She shrunk back behind a tree. What if Mr. Smith had an accomplice? She hadn't considered that, but that might explain why Mr. Smith was being so slow in doing anything to his victim. He was waiting for the accomplice, and they were probably both waiting for it to become completely dark.

Bunny couldn't be dissuaded that easily, though. She knew of a path where she could keep her eye on Mr. Smith and circle behind the accomplice. Maybe then she could find out what they were really up to.

*S*am had lucked out that Bunny was pulling out of her street when he drove over with Dooley. He'd decided to follow her and was surprised to see her turn into the Rachel Carson Wildlife Refuge. Was she just going birdwatching? He felt like a creepy stalker but followed her in anyway and parked in an out-of-the-way spot down the road to watch.

When she got out of her car with binoculars swinging on her neck, he'd almost left, but Dooley looked excited about the prospect of a walk in the woods, and Sam didn't see the harm in that. He grabbed his binoculars out of the back and got out of the car.

Sam took a different path from Bunny. He knew the wildlife refuge well and where each path intersected. Dooley was excited to sniff every leaf and blade of grass.

After walking a bit, Dooley pulled him over to a bench in the woods. The dog must have known Sam was getting a bit tired. He'd walked more in the past few days than he had in the past few years. From this vantage point, he could just see Bunny through his binoculars. She was sitting on a log, looking through her binoculars in the opposite direction.

Sam hadn't been there long when two men came walking down one of the paths. That was nothing unusual since the refuge was visited by many and it was a nice crisp fall evening. But what was unusual was that Bunny immediately trained her binoculars on the men.

Sam raised his own binoculars to follow their path. The two men sat on a bench and appeared to be having a friendly conversation. What in the world was that about? Was one of them the person Bunny had been surveilling when he'd seen her downtown with the newspaper? Was she some sort of private detective?

Perhaps he shouldn't be tailing her. He'd gotten a little overexcited, and the thought of having something to investigate had clouded his better judgment. The notion that Bunny Howard was some sort of suspect was preposterous. Maybe he just wanted something to do, and maybe he liked something about her, so finding out more about her couldn't hurt. Luckily, he hadn't done anything crazy, like bust out his old badge and accuse her of something.

But if she wasn't a suspect, why was she watching those men? She looked to be about his age. Maybe too old to be a private detective? Then again maybe not. Maybe he should consider becoming a private detective. He certainly did miss the thrill of the chase and had more than enough experience.

Dooley had been busying himself sniffing under a log. Sam reached down to pet him. "I should bring you here more often, huh?"

Dooley wagged his tail.

"Used to come here all the time with Jean," he said, as if to explain why he'd never brought the dog before. He glanced around, picturing all the trails he and Jean had walked. They used to stand under the oak tree over there and look at the marsh, trying to see who would be the first to spot a great blue heron. He could almost see the two of them now.

Those memories used to be clearer. Now they were fading. He closed his eyes as if to conjure up the

97

memory again, to embed it clearly in his mind, so it wouldn't disappear for good.

He could almost hear Jean's voice inside his head. "Keeping memories is good, but don't let them over-shadow everything you're doing now. Don't let old memories prevent you from moving on to make new ones."

Sam nodded. That advice sounded smart. It sounded just like something Jean would say. Maybe he *should* look into being a private detective and—

"Just what do you think you are doing?"

Sam's eyes snapped open, and he spun around to see Bunny Howard standing behind him. Her hands were fisted on her hips, her eyes were narrowed, and she was looking at him as if he were some sort of suspicious character.

Dooley wasn't much of a protector. He ran to the woman and nudged her hand as if wanting to be petted.

Much to Sam's surprise, Bunny complied, even smiling down at the dog.

"Dooley and I love coming to see the deer." He hadn't even thought to mention he used to come with Jean. Last week, that would have been the first thing that popped to mind. Maybe he was making progress. And oddly, he didn't feel guilty about not including his memories of Jean in his explanation. It was as if her words about moving forward without guilt were finally sinking in.

Bunny looked skeptical. "Usually, they're in the fields. You're in the middle of the woods."

That was true, but Sam chose to ignore her and ask his own question. "And what are you doing spying on those two men?" He pointed in the direction of the two men. They were barely visible through the cover of trees.

"You mean your cohorts?"

"What? I don't even know them." *Who says* cohorts *these days, anyway?*

"Of course you'd say that if you were up to something with them. I happen to know that the dark-haired one is very suspicious."

Sam smiled. She'd just admitted she was spying. "I'm not the one spying on them. Apparently you are. Why?"

Bunny hesitated. Dooley, whose gaze had been flicking back and forth between Sam and Bunny as if he were following the conversation, directed his attention to Bunny.

"Who are you anyway? Didn't I see you downtown the other day? Were you following Mr. Smith too?" she asked.

Ah, so the man's name is Mr. Smith. That answered one question, but there were still many to be answered.

Sam's detective instincts told him that Bunny didn't mean any harm, so he figured making friends was the best approach. Besides, he had to admit he was intrigued by this situation and, perhaps, a bit by her as well.

"I'm Sam Campbell. Just taking my dog for a walk here." Sam stuck out a tentative hand.

Bunny stared at it while making her decision then put her hand in his. Her hand was warm and soft, and she had a strong grip. "Bunny Howard."

"Nice to meet you, Bunny," Sam said as if he hadn't already known her name. "So, what is it that you think this Mr. Smith has done?"

Dooley had inched over toward Bunny and nudged her hand. She started petting him without hesitation. That was a good sign. Sam imagined Dooley was a good judge of character, and anyone who wouldn't hesitate to pet a dog couldn't be half bad.

"What is your interest in that?" Bunny kept petting Dooley as she cast a skeptical eye on Sam.

He supposed it was a fair question. "Nothing really. I just find it curious. I used to be a police detective, so I guess mysteries are in my blood."

Bunny's brows quirked up. "A detective? Well, in that case, I guess I could tell you. You see, it all started with the book club."

*D*espite her earlier suspicions, Bunny found herself warming to Sam. That was why she told him about how Mr. Smith had been lurking outside the book club meeting, how he'd smashed the cantaloupe on the cliff, and how he had a list of poisons. She omitted the part about Liz taking those out of the trash. She didn't want to get Liz into trouble.

And it didn't hurt that Sam was a retired detective. Maybe he'd know some good ways to figure out what Mr. Smith was up to and stop him if he was planning to harm someone. He was also kind of cute, and she really liked Dooley.

"So, when Liz said she overheard him saying he was meeting someone here, I felt like I should come here just to make sure he didn't have any nefarious plans for his companion. It can be very isolated here. A place where no one can hear you scream." Bunny looked around. The sun had set, but it was still light enough to see the trails. Even so, she'd better start back to her car soon.

Sam's brow quirked up. "No one can hear you scream?" He looked a little concerned.

"Oh sorry! I've been reading the new mystery book for the book club and might have been focusing on the tagline a bit too much. I guess I can be a bit overly dramatic sometimes."

Sam did not look surprised to hear that. "Well, it

sounds like you do have some valid concerns, and I suppose following this Smith character isn't doing any harm, but you should be careful."

"Oh, I will be." Bunny was a bit disappointed that Sam hadn't given her any sage detective advice. She was reluctant to end their chance meeting even though the dim light was starting to become worrisome and she wanted to get back to her car before it got too dark. But for some reason, she wanted to keep talking to Sam— probably because he hadn't given her any good advice yet on how to thwart Mr. Smith.

"This book club, is that the one at Tides?" Sam asked.

"Yes!" Bunny brightened. He'd heard of it. That was good. That meant he wasn't some random weirdo but a friend… or at least a friend of a friend.

Sam nodded. "Claire at Sandcastles told me about it."

"Oh, I love Sandcastles. Have you tried her cannoli?"

"Delicious. I love the blond brownies."

"Me too!"

"Dooley likes the Beach Bones."

"I'll bet."

"So, you like the book club then?" Sam asked.

"Well, we just had our first meeting, but it was fun. Lots of good snacks and good company." Bunny hesitated a bit, not wanting to sound too full of herself, before adding, "I was the only one who figured out who the killer was early on."

"Really? How fun." Sam seemed suitably impressed, as did Dooley.

"But I bet you'd be even better at it, seeing as you were a detective. You should join."

"I might." Sam stood. "It's getting rather late, and I don't think you're going to catch Mr. Smith doing anything tonight."

"Why is that?" Finally, this guy was going to impart some professional detective wisdom!

Sam nodded in the direction of the parking lot.

Bunny squinted and moved a branch aside to peer through the trees. Mr. Smith was walking to his car, his companion to another car. They waved and got in. Some detective she was—she hadn't even noticed they were leaving!

"Seems like they are both in good condition," Sam said.

"Oh, I guess that was just a regular meeting." Bunny felt a little silly.

"No worries. That doesn't mean that something funny isn't going on, just not tonight." Sam turned to her. "Can I walk you to your car?"

"Sure." They were both headed in the same direction anyway, so why not?

Luckily, the moon was full, and just enough light filtered through the tree branches to make the path easily navigable. They got to Bunny's car without incident.

"Well, it was nice meeting you and especially you, Dooley." Bunny bent down to pet the dog.

"Same here," Sam said. "So, what will you do next with the Mr. Smith situation?"

"Not sure. In the book I'm reading, the detective does a lot of following, but that hasn't worked out that good so far." Bunny looked up at Sam, who was a good foot taller than her. Now that they were in the open without the trees shadowing the moon, she could see he had lustrous silver hair and kind brown eyes. "Do you have any ideas?"

"I might have a few. What do you say we meet tomorrow at Sandcastles to discuss them?"

CHAPTER FOURTEEN

"*I*s that a truck from the hardware store?" Jane squinted past Andie to see out the dining room window at Tides.

"What? No. Why would the hardware truck be here? That's the food delivery. Brenda's stocking up." Andie grabbed her elbow and turned her toward the hallway. "Maybe you need glasses. Come over here. I want to show you something."

"I think Brenda might be overly optimistic about our bookings." Jane let Andie lead her to the back parlor. Why would they need another food delivery if they only had one guest and no new bookings?

One of the things Jane loved about Tides was that it had several common rooms for guests to gather in. It had once been the home of a sea captain and boasted several living rooms, a dining room, and smaller parlors.

There was plenty of room for guests to mingle in large groups as well as separate off into smaller more intimate groups.

The back parlor was a favorite because it had tall arched windows that faced the ocean. Right now, the view was stunning since the sun had risen about an hour ago and the sky was golden hued above the cobalt-blue ocean.

Andie plopped down on the couch and pointed at the coffee table, where there was a spread of pamphlets and magazines. "These are from the Antique Inn Conference."

Jane sat on the sofa on the other side of the coffee table. She picked up one of the pamphlets. It was nothing that exciting—some pictures of past conferences along with the booths and attendees. Another pamphlet had a list of the vendors who would be attending. "This is great."

Jane glanced back over her shoulder as she heard the truck drive off. "That was quick. Maybe Brenda isn't really that overly optimistic."

"Did you see the magazine?" Andie shoved a glossy magazine in front of her face. It had the name *Antique Inn Times* at the top and a picture of an old brick colonial. "These are other inns like ours. Maybe we should check some of them out."

"Do you think some of the other owners will be there? Might be good to talk to them."

"I hope so." Andie glanced at her watch. "Speaking of talking to people, we better get a move on over to Sandcastles. It's a gorgeous day to walk."

As they headed out the front door, Andie linked her arm through Jane's. "This trip is going to be really fun. I've even picked out a nice restaurant for us and booked us some spa time at the hotel."

Jane smiled at her sister. "That sounds great. Thanks for making all the arrangements."

Sandcastles was only a few blocks away, and they were seated at the table with Claire and Maxi sipping their coffees in no time. Andie had filled the walk with chatter about the hotel she'd booked, the restaurants, and other sights they might take in in Bar Harbor. Jane was getting excited about the trip, even if she was slightly nervous about leaving the inn. Mr. Smith probably wouldn't even notice she was gone, though. She hardly saw him, and any attempts to strike up a conversation were met with polite but very short replies.

"What is this?" Andie pointed to one of the pastries that Claire had loaded onto a plate in the middle of their table.

"Apple cider Danish," Claire said proudly.

"What's the filling?" Maxi pointed to the blob in the middle that looked like mustard.

"Curcumin-spiced marmalade."

Everyone made a face.

"Maybe you should stick to basics," Jane said. "Your stuff is already fantastic."

Claire sighed. "Thanks. But I wanted some new offerings for fall."

"Most of the ones we tested the other day were great. That seemed like plenty," Maxi said.

Jane nodded. "And everyone already loves your pastries. Even the town dogs. Speaking of which, remind me to get some Beach Bones for Cooper before I leave today. I'm dropping him off at Mike's this afternoon for our trip, and I want him to be stocked up."

"What's going on with those?" Maxi asked. "Did you ever find out who was using the name?"

Claire shook her head. "Nope. Maybe the customers were just mistaken, or the person stopped selling them. I'm not going to worry about it, and I'm definitely going to keep selling them. They've brought some new customers in and caused some old ones to keep returning." Claire nodded toward a table in the corner, and Jane looked to see an older man sitting alone, his head bent over the newspaper, pencil in hand.

"Isn't that Sam Campbell?" Jane asked.

"Yep. He gets the Beach Bones for Dooley. Dooley's out front," Claire said, and everyone swiveled their attention to the front door, where the beagle mix was tied to the post, waiting patiently.

"That's great. I haven't seen Sam around much the past few years since Jean…" Jane let her voice trail off and looked at the corner again. Sam looked content, and if she wasn't mistaken, his pale complexion had a bit of color in it now. He was also sitting straighter, less stooped, than when she'd last seen him.

"He's been coming in a lot more lately. I think Dooley has been good for him. He usually just gets a pastry for himself and the Beach Bones for Dooley and then leaves, but today, I guess he decided to sit for a while. It's good to see him getting back out."

The front door opened, and Bunny Howard came in. She looked smart in a yellow sunflower-splotched shirt and jeans, her hair carefully swept into her usual bun. She scanned the café, which was crowded, as usual, her gaze stopping at the corner table.

"Well, will you look at that," Maxi said. "Looks like maybe Sam came here for more than the pastries and Beach Bones this morning."

*B*unny had wondered if Sam would actually show up and was almost surprised when she recognized Dooley tied up outside. She wasn't sure why she was surprised. Sam hadn't struck her as the type of person who reneged on plans, but she still found it a bit unusual to make plans with someone she'd met in the woods. Well, she supposed that's what people did these days.

Sam was sitting in the corner. He had a coffee mug to his right and a newspaper laid out in front of him with a school-bus-yellow pencil hovering over it. Was he doing a crossword puzzle? Bunny's thoughts toward him warmed even more. She loved crosswords.

She hurried over to the corner, barely waving at Jane, Claire, and the others as she breezed past their table.

As she approached Sam's table, he looked up and smiled. Then surprisingly, he stood and pulled out a chair for her. *Who does that anymore?* Bunny took this as another indication that Sam was a good guy. He had manners, and maybe it was a bit old-fashioned, but so was she. Sam was a person she could be friends with, someone she could trust.

"Good morning. How are you today?" Sam asked.

"Wonderful." Bunny twisted around in her seat, looking for Hailey, because she really needed coffee.

Hailey was there in an instant, filling up her mug.

"Did you order anything to eat?" Bunny asked Sam.

Sam shook his head. "I was waiting for you. I didn't know if you would want anything."

"Are you kidding? I never turn down an opportunity to eat." Bunny looked up at Hailey. "I'll have a bran muffin."

Sam smiled. "I'll have the same. Oh, and a half dozen Beach Bones for Dooley."

Sam's gaze slid to the window, where he could see

the dog tied out front. Bunny could see how his eyes lit up when he saw the dog safe and happy out there.

"Claire's bran muffins are my favorite. I love the raisins, and do you know she puts real shredded carrot in them?" Sam asked.

"I do indeed. They're very good and not too sweet. I saw Dooley outside and gave him a little pat. He's a great dog."

"Thank you very much. He's good company."

Bunny nodded. She imagined he would be. She knew that Liz adored her new dog. *Maybe I should consider getting one myself.* Her gaze fell on the crossword. She tilted her head sideways to see the clues and what Sam had filled in so far.

"Risky," Bunny said.

Sam's left brow shot up. "Pardon?"

"Twelve down." Bunny pointed to the newspaper. "Full of uncertainty. Five letters."

"Oh!" Sam penciled it in. "Are you a fan of crosswords?"

"I am. Do them all the time." Bunny tapped the side of her head. "Keeps the brain active."

"I agree." Sam looked up, and their gazes met.

Bunny got the strange feeling that something important was happening. Then Hailey came with their muffins, and they got busy cutting them open and putting butter on. Bunny was amused to discover that Sam used an overabundance of butter, just like she did.

Sam cleared his throat. "Shall we get to the business at hand? Do you have any ideas of how to proceed with our little…" Sam glanced around and then lowered his voice. "Investigation."

Bunny frowned at the people at the next table. Were they eavesdropping? She leaned forward and lowered her voice. "Maybe we should come up with a code word. We don't need people overhearing us and assuming we're stalking someone or anything."

"Good idea. It could be risky"—Sam tapped the word on his crossword—"if people overhear us. In the police force, sometimes we'd make a code name for the suspect. What if we refer to our suspect as 'the dogcatcher?' People will think we are simply referring to the actual dogcatcher."

Bunny wasn't sure if Lobster Bay even had a dogcatcher, but she supposed it would work. No one would be interested in conversations about a dogcatcher. "Sounds good."

"So, what do you think our next steps should be?" Sam asked.

Bunny sat up a bit straighter. With his investigating experience, Sam was sure to have ideas on what to do next, but Bunny was proud he was asking her opinion.

"Well, I've gotten most of my ideas so far from the mystery book we're reading for the book club. This month's book is *Death on the Cliffs*, which coincidentally involves a mysterious death in a seaside town just like this. Anyway, the protagonist in this book gets most of the clues by following the suspect... er, dogcatcher... around, interviewing people about suspicious events. And she also breaks into his place. I'm not sure we should do that, though." Bunny pinched off the top of her muffin. "But you have real-life experience, so your ideas are probably much better."

"Not at all," Sam said. "I think you've got a great start. That's basically how I would do it. But I think we've already followed Mr., er... the dogcatcher... and we don't want to overdo it. Otherwise, he might notice."

Bunny pressed her lips together. "True. So, what do you suggest we do next?"

"Well, on the job, I used to do a lot of research into the background of someone we were looking into. I don't have access to the databases anymore. I probably wouldn't even know how to use them now." Sam laughed, and Bunny joined him.

Technology certainly had changed a lot, as Bunny had learned when she was shown a new program for digital painting a few weeks ago. The program was neat, but she wondered if she'd have the patience to use it. She was sure she could figure it out if she devoted the time to it, but why bother? She much preferred using paintbrushes and real paper.

Sam continued, "I think we can get some information just using the internet. Social media is so revealing these days."

"That's a great idea." Bunny wondered where they would do this. Of course, she had a computer at home, but it didn't seem right to invite Sam over. He seemed nice enough, but she barely knew the man. What if he was really some weirdo who gained access to ladies' homes by pretending to work with them? She'd read a book where that happened. "We could meet at the library and use the computers there."

"That's a wonderful idea," Sam said. "I suppose maybe we should exchange phone numbers just in case one of us can't make it."

"Yes, that would be a good idea. Plus, we can message each other if one of us gets an idea or finds a clue." Bunny pulled out her phone, and they exchanged numbers. "I prefer texting. How about you?"

"Me too. I'm not much of a phone talker."

"Well, this sounds like a good plan." Bunny looked regretfully at the empty muffin cup on her plate. She'd already had two cups of coffee and didn't want a third, yet she felt reluctant to leave. She did have that painting to work on at home, though.

"What time would you like to meet at the library?" Sam was looking at his empty plate too.

"How about three thirty?" That would give Bunny time to get her thoughts together, figure out what to search, and finish her painting.

"Sounds good."

Hailey brought the bill, and Sam insisted on paying.

"I wouldn't dream of letting you pay. You're helping me out," Bunny said.

"Not at all. I'm looking forward to doing something useful, so, in a way, you're helping *me* out." Sam pulled out his wallet.

"Oh well, since you put it that way. I'll get the next one, then," Bunny said.

"That sounds like a deal."

Bunny left Sandcastles with Sam's words ringing in her head. He was glad to be doing something useful. That was exactly how she felt about it. And if they stopped Mr. Smith from doing something horrible, that would be an added bonus.

CHAPTER FIFTEEN

"Well, this has been a busy day, hasn't it?" Sam said to Dooley later that day. After his meeting with Bunny at Sandcastles, he'd taken Dooley for a walk on the beach. Now they were back home in the dining room, where Sam was clearing some of the knickknacks off the tables.

He glanced over at Dooley as if looking for an answer, but the dog was staring into the kitchen, his gaze riveted on the counter, where Sam had put the bakery bag of Beach Bones.

"Oh, I see, you have other things on your mind." Sam took one of the bones out of the bag, broke it in half, tossed it to Dooley, then returned to the dining room.

"I think these will be much better in the curio cabinet." Sam wasn't much of a knickknack guy. Jean had collected all of these little glass figures, frogs, fish, dogs —you name it. She'd placed them on various tables and windowsills around the house. She hadn't overdone it so it didn't look cluttered, and the figures were cute, but Sam though it was time for a cleaner look.

He didn't want to toss them away—that would be like tossing Jean away—so he moved them to the curio cabinet, arranging them carefully in a way he thought she would like. When he was done, he stood back and smiled. At first, he'd thought doing this might make him sad, but as it turned out, it only did a teeny bit. Mostly, it felt right. This way, the main parts of the house would be a little less about her and a little more about him.

"It's about time I make the place my own, don't you think?"

"Woof." Dooley seemed to agree. Or maybe he just wanted another bone.

"You don't think I should have invited her over here, do you?"

Dooley tilted his head as of considering the question.

Sam hadn't really known what to suggest to Bunny when it came to continuing their investigation, but it seemed a bit awkward to invite her to his house. Was he being too old-fashioned? It wasn't like they were going on dates; they were investigating a suspect.

But was Mr. Smith really a suspect? His detective instincts told him probably not, but still, there was no harm in what they were doing. And Bunny had said something that struck home… She'd said it made her feel useful. And that was exactly how it made Sam feel. Not to mention that he enjoyed Bunny's company. And she did crosswords! Since Jean had died, it seemed most of their friends had drifted away. About time Sam got some new ones.

Sam glanced at the clock. "Sorry, you can't come to the library."

Dooley padded over to the plush dog bed Sam had bought for him and made a show of lying down as if trying to tell Sam he preferred to take a nap anyway.

Sam grabbed the book of extra-difficult crossword puzzles from the pile on the end table in the den. *Let's see Bunny try to solve these,* he thought.

Out in the garage, he glanced at the Corvette still sitting under the tarp. It had been there a long time. Maybe he should at least wash and wax it. He reached out then pulled his hand back. *No, better to leave it covered.*

His convertible days were over. Besides, he was much more interested in this new investigation than in driving around in a flashy car anyway.

CHAPTER SIXTEEN

"*D*on't forget to bring a jacket. It's going to be colder in Bar Harbor," Andie instructed into the phone as if Jane didn't know that Bar Harbor was much farther north and, thus, colder.

"Yes, Mom." Jane switched the phone to her other hand as she leaned into the car to grab the bag of things for Cooper that she was bringing to Mike's. He already had his own basket of toys, dog beds, treats, and food at Mike's, but for some reason, Jane felt like she should bring more. It might have been the slight guilt at leaving him for the weekend trip with Andie. She hadn't left Lobster Bay since meeting Mike and Cooper.

"Very funny."

Jane could hear the bell in Andie's shop tinkle, announcing a customer, then Andie said, "Okay, catch you later. I'll pick you up bright and early tomorrow."

Jane hung up and tugged Cooper to Mike's front door. Mike lived in an upscale townhouse with crisp white vinyl siding and gray shutters. It had a nice backyard for Cooper and great landscaping throughout the development.

"You're going to miss me, right?" She glanced down at Cooper. His silky blond tail wagged, and his soulful brown eyes gazed up at her. "I'll take that as a yes."

She knocked on the door. She had a key but still felt a little funny just walking in. When Mike didn't answer after a few seconds, she rang the bell.

Footsteps echoed, and then he answered. His hair was a bit messy, and... were those wood chips in it?

"Hi," he said.

"Hi. Were you in the basement?" Jane peered into his place, expecting to see signs of a home renovation project. Was he changing things in preparation to ask her to move in?

"What? No. I mean, yes. The breaker went." He stood back and opened the door for them to enter then crouched down to pet Cooper, who wriggled, basking in the attention.

"The breaker? This place is brand-new. You wouldn't think there would be electrical issues." Jane felt like Mike was acting a bit suspicious, but why? Did this have something to do with her ring suspicions? What would a ring have to do with electricity?

"It's fine. I was just doing too much. Air fryer was

on, plus I was fixing a table leg for Judy and was using tools." Mike motioned toward the basement.

Judy was Mike's neighbor, a nice older woman he often did little maintenance tasks for.

Maybe Jane was reading too much into this. With the book club mysteries, Mr. Smith, and her ring suspicions, she really was probably overreacting. A weekend away with Andie would help to clear her head.

She relaxed and smiled as Mike took the bag of Cooper's gear and gave her a kiss. Cooper had made his way to his toy basket and was snuffling inside for a toy.

"Are you excited about your trip?" Mike asked.

"Yeah. A bit." She was excited, but also a bit apprehensive. "I'm going to miss you."

Mike smiled and kissed the tip of her nose. "Miss you too. But you know they say absence makes the heart grow fonder."

Cooper selected a stuffed octopus from the basket and dropped it at Jane's feet.

"Looks like someone wants to play," Mike said.

"Woof!"

"Why don't you take Coop outside, and I'll make us a few cups of coffee, and we can toss the toy around in the backyard."

Mike had recently fenced in the yard, and they'd spent several weekend mornings and evenings outside with Cooper.

"Sounds good." Jane picked up the toy. Cooper

knew the drill and rushed to the back door before she'd even straightened up. It was a familiar routine. Perfectly normal.

"Girl, you gotta get a grip on your overactive imagination," Jane muttered to herself as she tossed the octopus toward the back corner of the yard.

CHAPTER SEVENTEEN

*T*he Lobster Bay Library was housed in a big stone building with a giant oak door that had side iron hinges and looked like it belonged on an old castle. Bunny thought the door was so interesting that she'd even made a painting of it once.

A cement path lined with colorful flowers led to the door. The pink and white impatiens were still blooming even this late in the season, and there were gorgeous pots of mums in bright yellow and deep purple.

Inside, the space was cloaked in hushed silence. The walls were painted the palest shade of blue, and the royal-blue carpeting muted Bunny's footsteps.

Evelyn Carson was seated behind the round desk opposite the door. She looked up over her red-framed half-moon glasses and smiled at Bunny. Evelyn had been town librarian for decades and always had a kind word for everyone who entered. Unless people talked too loudly, then she would shush them sternly.

"Pssst..." Bunny turned toward the sound to see Sam sitting in one of the wingback chairs over by the fireplace.

She waved, and he stood and walked over to her.

"I hope you haven't been waiting long." Bunny hated being late, so she had shown up five minutes early. Sam must not like being late either, she surmised. Another thing they had in common.

"Not at all. I was returning a book anyway and figured I'd catch you when you came in and we could walk down to the computer area together."

The computers were kept in the back of the library, in a small room with utilitarian wooden desks and uncomfortable plastic chairs. They were older models, and back when no one had home computers, the room was used often. But these days, everyone had a laptop, and Bunny had actually brought hers. The room was a bit dusty and seemed like no one had been in it for a while, but it was a good place to meet. They'd also be able to discuss the investigation in privacy without risking Evelyn's shushing or anyone spying on their activities.

Bunny put her laptop on one of the desks, and they pulled two chairs over.

"I guess we can start by searching Google?" Bunny raised a brow at Sam.

"Yep. Good a place as any." Now that Sam was sitting closer to her than at Sandcastles, she noticed the crinkles around his eyes from laughing and also that his eyes were blue. He smelled good, too, clean like soap.

"Oh!" Sam pulled something out of his jacket pocket. "Almost forgot. I brought you this crossword puzzle book. These are quite difficult."

Bunny slid her reading glasses on, feeling almost a bit self-conscious because she noticed Sam didn't have reading glasses. Maybe his eyes were still good. Well, that was okay. She was happy for him.

"I don't think I've tried these. Thanks." She put the book in her bag, confident she could solve the puzzles in record time.

As her fingers flew over the keyboard, she noticed the flecks of blue and brown paint. Sam did too.

"Were you painting your house?" he asked.

Bunny laughed. "No, I'm an artist. I was painting a vignette of shells before I came here."

"An artist? Wow, that's impressive. Do you have any pictures of your paintings?"

Bunny felt a flush of pride. Sam seemed genuinely interested. "Well, I suppose I have a few on my phone."

She practically knocked her bag off the table, getting to her phone. She opened one of her photo albums and scrolled through a few pictures for Sam. Not too many, though—she didn't want to be one of those boring people who showed dozens of pictures when a few would suffice.

"Is that a moon snail shell? You captured the colors so perfectly. A lot of people think those shells are too plain to be admired, but they are actually quite lovely," Sam said.

"I totally agree." Bunny put away her phone.

"Thanks for showing me those. You're very talented."

"Oh, well…" Bunny stammered, suddenly feeling self-conscious. "Thank you. I guess we should get started. Do you want to drive?" Bunny slid the laptop in front of Sam.

"Sure. What's our, er… dogcatcher's… first name?"

"Reginald." Liz had looked that up in the guest book at Bunny's request.

"Oh, good. That's a bit unusual, so that will make it easier. I was afraid you were going to say something like Bob. There must be a dozen Bob Smith's everywhere."

They spent the next hour googling, searching Facebook, and even looking into Instagram. But they came up with absolutely nothing for a Reginald Smith who lived in Greenville, New Hampshire.

"Well, I guess we've exhausted all our avenues." Sam stared at the computer thoughtfully. "Are you sure Liz got the town right?"

"I can ask her." Bonnie closed the laptop. "So, what's the next step?"

"If I was still on the job, we'd interview people close to the subject. But we don't really know anyone close to Mr. Smith."

"Just Jane and Liz, but they don't really *know* him." Bunny shoved the laptop into her bag. "I've already asked Liz about him, and from what she says, he's a bit mysterious. Keeps to himself."

They sat there for a few seconds, both thinking. Bunny was reluctant to get up and leave, and she wondered if Sam felt the same.

"Perhaps we should arrange a time to meet again after we've thought about this. I can fill you in on what Liz says after I talk to her." Bunny tapped the side pocket of her tote, where she'd put the crossword puzzles. "And I can fill you in on how easy these were."

Sam laughed. "Good idea. Shall we walk out together?"

Near the front of the room was a kiosk with the book display. One of them was *Death on the Cliffs*, the next book club book. "Oh, this is the next book we're reading for the book club."

Sam picked up the book and leafed through a few pages. "Claire asked if I wanted to join the club. I just might."

"You should! It's a lot of fun. I like to play along with the detective, kind of like solving a real crime. There are lots of ideas on how to catch killers. Like in the last book, the killer invited his victim to a somewhat-public place but at a time when he knew they would be alone." Bunny looked thoughtful. "That's why I thought the dogcatcher was up to something when he brought that other person to the Rachel Carson Refuge."

"That would be a good place to do someone in. Lots of places to hide a body in there. Of course, the cliffs on a remote beach or a creepy old inn on the water would be a good place too."

Bunny laughed. "The beaches here are hardly remote. Always someone walking along the Marginal Way, and Mr.... er... the dogcatcher would hardly be alone at Tides."

"Right. Of course. He must be planning something else... *if* he is planning anything."

Bunny sensed Sam was doubtful about Mr. Smith. Did he think she was being foolish? If so, he was being a good sport about going along with her. If nothing else, it was kind of fun and gave them something to do.

Her spirits picked up even further when he tucked the book under his arm and headed toward the checkout desk. Maybe he would join the book club. She wouldn't mind having an excuse to see Sam on a regular basis. It was always nice to have a friend with similar interests.

CHAPTER EIGHTEEN

*C*laire balanced one of her specialty sandcastle-shaped cakes in her left hand while she opened the door to the display case with her right. She slid the cake carefully onto the middle shelf and stood back to admire her handiwork. The cake was one of her biggest yet, with two turrets and a moat. She'd covered the structure in sand-colored sugar, and the moat was blue frosting.

She closed the door and turned in time to see Sam Campbell tying Dooley up to the post outside. Sam patted the dog's head then stood and walked into the store. His back was straight, his head high. No more shuffling, and was that a smile on his face?

"Hi, Sam. Back for more Beach Bones?" Claire hurried behind the counter.

"Yes, please. Dooley loves them. And also a bran muffin for myself."

"How are you today?"

"Just fine. It's a warm afternoon, and I'm taking Dooley for a walk on the beach. He loves it, and it's been far too long that I haven't been doing that."

Claire simply looked up and smiled. She couldn't have agreed more. She noticed the book tucked under his arm. "That's the book for the book club. Are you thinking about joining?"

"Yes, I was at the library with Bunny Howard earlier, and she mentioned this was the book. I remember you had invited me, and I thought maybe it's time for me to get out a bit more."

"Bunny, huh?" Claire's gaze slid to the table where she'd seen Sam and Bunny earlier. Apparently, they'd hit it off. That was good. "She's a character, isn't she?"

Sam laughed. "She sure is."

"We'd love to have you at the book club. It meets the last Thursday of every month at Tides. Just show up around seven if you want to come."

"I think I will. Thank you." Sam paid for the bag, and Claire noticed a spring in his step as he left.

"I bought some of these Beach Bones in a cute little shop over in Kennebunkport!" Two women who had come in while Claire had been waiting on Sam were standing in front of the case. "I'm glad to see she's branching out and selling them in your shop too."

Claire frowned. "What do you mean? I make these dog treats here."

The woman squinted and leaned closer to the case. "Really? I bought dog bones just like this in a cute little gift store over in Kennebunkport, and I swear they were called Beach Bones." The woman opened her large tote bag and rummaged around. She pulled out the little bag tied up in a blue ribbon. It had a card on it and two gourmet dog bones that looked just like Claire's inside. She held it out toward Claire. "Yep. See? Beach Bones."

The woman with her regarded Claire with suspicion. "I was there too. Didn't that other woman say someone was copying her?"

"What?" Claire was offended. "I'm not copying her! I made them first." Or did she? She might have made them first, but she hadn't named them until earlier that week. Was it possible she'd inadvertently used the same name as someone else?

The woman looked skeptical. "Well, I don't think I'm going to buy yours. I saw this lady's first, so I don't know if she is the original or you are."

"Can I see that card?" Claire hoped she'd find the person's name on the back. Maybe she could contact them and settle the whole thing.

The woman handed her the package. Sure enough, a name was on the back of the card. Claire did a double take when she saw who it was. "Oh no. Anyone but her."

CHAPTER NINETEEN

"I don't know why we had to leave so early," Jane said to Andie as they drove up the turnpike. It was just before eight in the morning, and she'd barely taken a sip of her coffee. "We can't even check in until three."

"I figured we could take the scenic route and stop at a few places. There's a cute lobster shack with a great view and outstanding clam chowder on the way." Andie sounded annoyingly peppy. She must really be looking forward to this conference. "The leaves are starting to change farther north. Should be pretty."

"I suppose that sounds nice." Jane took another sip of coffee, her thoughts returning to when she'd dropped Cooper off at Mike's. He'd acted mostly normal, except for that strange part about him not being in the basement. Was he doing something down there? But if so, what did that have to do with an engagement ring? Or was her hunch about that off base? Jane decided it was best to not say anything to anyone. It would be really embarrassing if she assumed he was up to that and it turned out he wasn't.

"Are you worried about leaving Tides? It will be fine," Andie said.

"It just seems weird to leave a guest there alone."

"He has a key, and Brenda will be there tomorrow morning to feed him. He seemed fine with it."

"But what if someone walks in and wants to book a room?"

"Seriously? No one has done that in weeks. It's not summertime, and anyway, we left that big sign on the check-in desk with our phone numbers, and Liz said if we get someone last minute, she'll run over and get them set up." Andie glanced at her. "Are you worried that Mr. Smith might have a party and wreck the place like an unsupervised teenager?"

Jane laughed. Andie had a point—she was probably worrying too much. "No, but he did ask if he could have that friend over."

"Really? That's kind of funny. Of course anyone can come over."

Jane settled back in her seat and watched the passing scenery. Andie seemed quite at ease with leaving Tides unattended, but still, she sensed a bit of tension thrumming along underneath her sister's calm demeanor.

Maybe it was just excitement over the conference, or maybe it was something else. Visions of Andie and Mike seemingly doing something behind her back and her mother's mention of the dimensions and size bubbled up.

It was probably all her imagination. Reading the mystery books for the book club had certainly renewed her interest in mysteries. But if there really was something going on, this trip with her sister might be the perfect time to try to wheedle some information out of her.

CHAPTER TWENTY

*B*unny called Liz as soon as she got home from her library meeting with Sam. She was eager to ask Liz if she could have been wrong about Mr. Smith's town of residence, but that wasn't going to happen right away since Liz was busy. They made plans for the following afternoon, and Bunny occupied her time with the crossword puzzles Sam had given her.

Sam was right—they were challenging. Still, Bunny had made good progress that night, and when she awoke in the morning, she finished three of them while having a cup of coffee. They weren't *that* hard.

She couldn't wait to tell Sam, so she messaged him: *Crosswords are a piece of cake! Completed the first three already.*

After a few minutes, she got a reply: *Good work. Try the one on page 98. That's a doozy.*

Sam was right. It *was* a doozy. After working on it for a few hours, Bunny decided to get to her painting. She'd finished the one with the shells and had started a seascape with waves crashing on the rocks.

She mixed up some shades of brown using burnt umber, yellow ochre, and white and started painting the rocks using the side of her palette knife to replicate the sharp edges.

Over the next few hours, she only took a few breaks to check her phone to see if Sam had messaged her again. Not that she was waiting around for him to strike up a conversation or invite her out or anything. They already had plans to meet again tomorrow after she talked to Liz, but she couldn't resist checking in, just in case he'd thought up something new they should try. Apparently, he hadn't, since no further texts came.

She was setting out some molasses cookies and getting the kettle ready for tea when she heard Liz tapping on the slider door.

Bunny rushed over to open it. "Come on in. I baked some cookies."

"Oh, you didn't have to do that!" Liz stopped at the painting. "How lovely!"

Bunny felt a flush of pride. "Thanks!"

Liz stepped into the kitchen, her eyes widening at the plate of cookies. She sniffed the air. "Bunny, these smell amazing!"

Bunny inhaled the aroma of sugar, spice, and

molasses as she turned up the burner under the kettle. "I love baking—it's so therapeutic for me."

Liz took a seat at the table and reached for a cookie. "Don't let Claire find out. She might get worried."

Bunny laughed as she fixed the tea. "I doubt that, but it's still fun. So, what have you been up to?"

Liz smiled. "I was busy mailing some things I found in the basement to my sister and brother."

Liz was still cleaning stuff out from her childhood home and often sent some of the sentimental discoveries to her siblings.

"That's nice. I'm sure they appreciate that." Bunny sat at the table and dipped her tea bag into the mug of steaming water. Normally, she loved this neighborly chitchat, but today, she wanted to get right to the point.

"And I had another little errand." Liz took her time adding sugar and cream to the tea. Bunny was almost ready to prompt her when she said, "I stopped by the animal rescue to look at the dogs."

"You did! Oh, that's so exciting. Did you get one?"

Liz shook her head. "No, not yet."

"How come?"

Liz sighed. "I want to adopt the perfect dog, and there are so many to choose from! I've been going every day to visit them, and I just can't make up my mind."

"I know exactly how you feel. I've thought about getting one, too, but I'm not sure exactly what kind I should get." Bunny thought about Dooley. She wanted a dog just like Dooley. He was quiet, obedient, and lovable.

"So anyway, enough about me. What's going on with you? Did I hear you had a date?"

Bunny snorted. "A date? Hardly. I've been working on finding out more about Mr. Smith with a detective friend, Sam."

"Oh? Wow, I guess you really suspect him of something. If a detective is involved, I'm worried he might be dangerous."

"Oh no, dear, it's not like that." Bunny didn't want Liz to worry. "Sam is a retired detective. We're not sure, just looking into him. Which reminds me—I have a question."

"Oh?" Liz raised a brow and sipped her tea.

"Are you quite sure that Mr. Smith is from Greenville, New Hampshire?"

Liz pressed her lips together and thought for a few seconds. "I think so. I mean, that's what he put on the register."

"Did you ask him or hear him mention the town?"

"No. You don't think he'd be lying, do you?"

Bunny shrugged. "I don't know why he would."

"Huh, well, he sure is an odd duck. Speaking of Tides, I hope Andie and Jane are having a good time."

"What do you mean? Is something going on at Tides?"

"Oh no. Well, yes, but what I meant was that Andie

and Jane are out of town at a convention and doing some sister bonding."

"Oh, that's nice. So do you have to go over and stay at Tides?"

"Nope. Jane said there's a key for Mr. Smith, and he wasn't planning on going out anyway."

"Wait. You mean Mr. Smith is at Tides all alone tonight?"

"Oh no, he isn't all alone. He asked Jane and Andie if he could have someone over to visit."

Bunny's heart lurched. She reached for her phone to message Sam. She didn't say anything to Liz because she didn't want to worry her, but she had a terrible feeling that they needed to get over there right away before something bad happened!

CHAPTER TWENTY-ONE

"*I* think this will make a perfect den, don't you?" Sam asked Dooley. They were standing in one of the extra bedrooms. Jean had used it for a sewing room, but Sam didn't sew, and it was a waste to leave it set up.

He'd been happy to give the sewing machine to one of his neighbors and even happier to actually connect with the neighbor. Turns out the people who had moved in across the street were a nice younger couple with not a lot of money. She loved sewing outfits for their twin girls and really appreciated the sewing machine.

Thoughts about that interaction and the texts from Bunny made Sam smile. He'd figured Bunny would be able to finish the crosswords easily. She'd probably started from the beginning. Those were fairly straightforward, but what she didn't know was that they got more difficult toward the back. He couldn't wait to see how she did with the one on page ninety-eight.

He stood back to look at the room. He'd replaced the sewing table beside the window with a cozy armchair that was perfect for reading. A small desk where he could use his computer sat in the corner. It was perfect.

"Now time to have a rest." Dooley glanced expectantly toward the kitchen.

"I guess you want a treat before resting?"

"Woof!" Dooley raced to the kitchen.

Sam got a biscuit out of the tin and made a coffee. As he was stirring in creamer, he spotted the book club book on the kitchen table. He'd started it earlier in the day, and it was quite intriguing. Now would be a perfect time to relax in the den and read a few more chapters.

Dooley followed him into the den and got settled in the plush dog bed Sam had put in the corner.

"This fellow really is quite clever." Of course there were a few things in the book that weren't realistic, but Sam expected that. Making all the police red tape and rules true to life would make for a pretty boring novel. But he had to admit the author knew his stuff.

Sam looked at the author bio on the back of the book. The author picture was interesting. It was mostly in shadow, which made it difficult to make out the guy's face. It definitely set the mood, though, with the author dressed in a hat and trench coat like an old-time detective.

"I wonder what other books this guy has written." Sam put the book on the side table and sat at the computer to google the author's name.

"Huh, Pat Jamison... Looks like he has quite a few books." Sam clicked on one of the links, and a listing of books and a better picture of the author came up. Sam squinted at the picture.

"Well, I'll be..." He reached for his phone then realized he'd left it in the kitchen while rearranging the den. "I need to message Bunny right away!"

But when he picked up his phone, he saw Bunny had messaged him. His heart dropped.

Meet me at Tides right away. The dogcatcher might be ready to make a move!

The text had been sent thirty minutes ago. Sam grabbed his keys and rushed to the garage. "Hold down the fort, Dooley. I have to stop Bunny from doing something drastic!"

CHAPTER TWENTY-TWO

"*T*his lobster bisque is amazing." Andie gestured toward the bowl of creamy pink soup in front of her. "Want to try some?"

They were seated at a window table at an upscale waterfront restaurant. The view of the harbor at night was mesmerizing, from the boats swaying on the water to the lights of the buildings behind them to the reflection of the moon.

The table was covered in a crisp white tablecloth, and the wineglasses sparkled with reflections from the electric candles on the table.

"Thanks." Jane dipped her spoon in and tasted it—rich and creamy, just like it looked. "Delish."

Andie sighed and took a sip of her wine. "This is a great restaurant. I'm glad we got to spend the weekend together. I thought the conference was really good. Did you?"

"I did. I'm glad we came." The Antique Inns Conference had been a lot more informative than Jane had anticipated. She'd connected with several antique inn owners from various parts of New England and gotten some ideas for promotions they could do to attract more visitors.

"Me too." Andie dug into her lobster casserole.

Jane studied her sister. Was it her imagination, or had Andie been evasive when she mentioned Mike earlier that day? If Jane wanted to dig into what was really going on, this would be the perfect time, especially if Andie had another glass of wine.

"So, I was wondering, have you noticed that Mike is acting a little strange?"

Andie looked up sharply. "Strange? No. What do you mean?"

Jane shrugged. "I don't know. He just seems a little off lately."

Andie frowned and took another sip of wine. "You think so? I hadn't noticed."

"Really?" Jane set down her spoon. "I thought maybe you had. I saw you talking to him the other morning at Tides."

"I talk to him a lot, but I didn't notice anything. He still seems just as smitten with you as ever." Andie shrugged and took another bite of her casserole.

Jane watched her sister for a moment longer then picked up her fork and picked some stuffing out of her baked stuffed shrimp. Maybe she was just being paranoid. "It's not that I think he's losing interest in me. Quite the opposite, actually."

"The opposite? What do you think is going on with him?" Andie asked casually. Almost *too* casually.

Jane paused with her fork halfway to her mouth. "Well, I know it might be presumptuous, but I was visiting Mom the other day, and she said Mike had been there asking about dimensions, but I think she really meant size." Jane pointed to her ring finger.

Andie's eyes widened. "You mean you think he might be looking for a ring for you?"

"Maybe. I don't know." Jane was starting to regret bringing this up, especially since Andie had a funny smirk on her face. She'd figured that maybe Mike had asked for Andie's advice, but now she wasn't so sure.

"Well, I wouldn't put much weight on what Mom says. She does have dementia." Andie sipped more wine, sat back in her seat, and studied Jane. "But if he was looking for a ring, would you be happy or disappointed?"

Jane wasn't sure which she would be. "Nervous."

Now Andie was looking at her with a knowing expression that spoke volumes. Mike *was* shopping for a ring. Jane could tell just from the look on Andie's face. She really didn't know how she felt. On the one hand, she didn't want to lose him, but on the other, she just wasn't ready.

A sense of doom came over her as she wondered when Mike was going to spring this on her, and when he did... what was she going to say?

CHAPTER TWENTY-THREE

unny approached Tides from the beach like she had when she'd attended the book club. The salty air whipped at her face, and she pulled her hood up to protect herself from the cold. It was getting dark, and she felt a tiny bit uncomfortable as she kept her eye on the dunes, looking for the three-story Victorian house.

"There's nothing to be worried about out here," she reassured herself. The killer was *inside* Tides, so the beach was safe. But even so, she was a little uneasy as she continued on. She felt Mr. Smith wouldn't expect someone to approach from the beach, and she wanted the element of surprise.

The lights on the main floor of Tides were on, and Bunny crept closer to the house, keeping to the shadows lest Mr. Smith be peeking out. She could hear what sounded like sawing somewhere on the back side of the house. Odd, because she assumed Mr. Smith would be alone with his victim. Did he have accomplices? No, maybe that was just the television. She cocked her ear to listen, but the sound of the waves crashing on the beach behind her drowned out almost everything.

Skirting along the edge of the building, she tiptoed up onto the porch, crossing her fingers that the boards wouldn't creak. She peeked out from the shadows just as someone passed the window. It was Mr. Smith! She jumped back. It wouldn't do to let him see her now.

He had someone with him. Was it the same man he'd met at the Rachel Carson Refuge? Bunny couldn't be sure. It didn't matter, though. Whoever it was, Bunny had to save them.

They headed into the side parlor, and Bunny inched over to the French doors. She reached out to touch the handle and tried turning it ever so slowly. It was locked!

Mr. Smith passed the doorway. He had something in his hand, and it looked like a knife!

Bunny's heart lurched. She had to get inside. She ran to the front, hoping the foyer door was open. It was!

She rushed inside, barely aware there was a lot of noise coming from the back of the house. She was more interested in the side where Mr. Smith was. She hurried through the dining room, down the hall, and through the door to the side parlor.

"Stop right there!" she yelled, then she hesitated in the doorway, confused about what to do next.

She'd been ready to tackle Mr. Smith and stop him from stabbing his victim, but she hadn't been expecting to see what was in front of her.

Mr. Smith and his victim were seated facing each other, a pile of books, two glasses of wine, and a tray of cheese and crackers sitting between them. They were both looking at her with startled expressions. Mr. Smith did have a knife, but he was using it to cut a slice of cheese.

She heard someone coming up behind her. "Yes! Stop!"

She whirled around.

Sam? What was he doing here, and why was he holding up the book club book?

Before she could say anything, he grabbed her elbow and escorted her into the room.

"Mr. Jamison, we were wondering if you'd be so kind as to sign our book."

Mr. Smith's concerned look morphed into a smile. "Very astute. I see you figured out who I am. I'd be delighted to sign it."

*B*unny played along with the whole thing. Apparently, Sam had researched the author of the book club book and recognized him as Mr. Smith. Bunny felt like she'd made a rookie mistake in not doing that herself.

The man with him was Steven Thompson, his agent —not a victim, as Bunny had suspected. Mr. Jamison had invited his agent to Tides to discuss a release date for his next book and sign some copies of the last one.

"I decided to come here in the off-season so I could have peace and quiet. I need to immerse myself when I'm writing," Mr. Jamison said.

"That makes perfect sense." Bunny nibbled on a cracker. "But I thought I saw you on the cliffs at the beach with a cantaloupe."

"I thought the beach was empty when I did that. It was research for the book. Now I can't tell you exactly what. Don't want to give away any spoilers." He winked at Bunny.

"And your trip to the hardware store?" Bunny asked. She didn't dare mention the list of poisons that Liz had found in his trash, but it made sense that that was probably research as well.

"Yep. More research."

"But why register here as Mr. Smith?" Bunny persisted.

Jamison grimaced. "I know it sounds pretentious,

but I need peace and quiet to write. Whenever I go anywhere and use my real name, word gets out, and next thing you know, people are showing up in the lobby and following me around."

"That must be terrible." Bunny took another cracker. She felt a little silly knowing the truth. She was glad that Mr. Smith, er... Jamison wasn't a killer, but it was a bit embarrassing that she'd just spent the last week following him around thinking nefarious thoughts. Luckily, he hadn't noticed.

"To tell you the truth, it was a bit of a surprise to discover that they were having a book club meeting about my book here. I couldn't help but lurk in the hallway and try to overhear what you all thought." Jamison looked apologetic as he signed Sam's book with a flourish and handed it over.

"We all loved it," Bunny said truthfully.

"It's much appreciated." Jamison smiled.

Bunny slid a piece of cheese onto another cracker, her attention drifting to the sounds of banging at the back of the house. *What in the world is going on back there?*

"Bunny! What are you doing here?" Liz had appeared in the doorway.

"Oh, umm... just getting a book signed."

Liz frowned at the books on the table then at Mr. Smith. She seemed confused, probably because she didn't know Mr. Smith's true identity. "Oh."

"What are you doing here, and what is going on out back?" Bunny asked.

"It's a surprise for Jane. Do you want to see?"

"Of course." Bunny grabbed another cracker and stood, motioning for Sam to join her.

"Okay, but I'll have to swear you to secrecy. Mike is surprising Jane when she gets back from her trip tomorrow."

Bunny promised not to tell and followed Liz down the hallway toward the back room where they'd had the book club meeting. She hung back a little bit and whispered to Sam, "Thanks for saving my butt."

He smiled. "No problem. That's what friends are for."

Bunny nodded. "Oh, by the way, the puzzle on page ninety-eight was a piece of cake."

CHAPTER TWENTY-FOUR

*a*ndie was chattering away as she drove the backroads back to Tides. If Jane didn't know better, she'd say her sister was nervous, but why would she be?

"Are you that excited to be home? You're rambling on like you used to do when we were kids and Mom and Dad took us for a car ride." Jane thought for a second. "Oh wait, that was because you had to pee."

"Ha ha. Very funny. I don't have to pee, and it's good to be home." Andie pulled into the driveway in front of Tides.

"Okay, well then you can just drop me off if you're in a hurry to get to your place." She was probably excited because she was meeting Shane.

"Oh no! I want to come in. I'm starving, and I have

nothing at home. Brenda probably has something delicious in the kitchen."

"Oh, okay."

Andie parked, and Jane pulled her suitcase out of the back while her sister ran in ahead. She must really be hungry, or she actually really did have to pee. Maybe Jane was overtired, but she had the feeling something odd was going on.

She was halfway to the staircase when Andie's voice rang out from somewhere in the back of the house. "Jane, you'd better come back here."

What the heck? Jane left her suitcase in the foyer and headed toward the kitchen, but Andie wasn't in there. "Where are you?"

"In the back hallway, down at the book club room."

The book club room? What in the world had made Andie go down there?

On no! Does this have something to do with Mike? Andie was in on whatever was going on—Jane was sure about it.

Jane got more nervous the closer she got to the book club room. Was that the murmuring of voices? It sounded like more than two people.

What's going on? Is Mike going to propose in front of a bunch of people? The thought made Jane want to run. Not that she didn't love Mike, but it was too soon. She wasn't sure if she'd say yes, and that would be especially awkward with a room full of witnesses.

But surely Andie would have told her given their conversation about it at the restaurant. Wasn't there some sister code that dictated she spill the beans even if she'd promised Mike to keep the secret? But then Andie had acted kind of smug, as if Jane's assumption was wrong.

There was only one way to find out. Jane forced a smile on her face as she turned the corner that led to the book club room.

"Surprise!"

Jane's jaw dropped. But not because Mike was kneeling in front of her with a shiny diamond ring. The room had been transformed into a library. Mahogany shelves ran from floor to ceiling. The old furniture had been replaced with leather Chesterfield sofas and club chairs. It was exactly what she and her dad had always envisioned.

Mike stood on the other side, beaming.

Jane beamed back. "You did this?"

"I had a little help." Mike gestured to the others in the room: Andie, Shane, Maxi, James, Claire, and Rob. Bunny and Sam were there, too, along with Liz and Brenda, of course. "Everyone helped."

"You guys did all this behind my back? But how?" Jane asked.

"It wasn't easy," Mike said. "Andie and I had to do some fast talking to get around your suspicious interrogations."

"Wait. So when I came over to your house, you were working on these shelves?" Jane remembered the sawdust.

"Yep."

"And when I thought I saw you both together here the other morning, that was true. And you *were* at the hardware store together."

"Right again," Andie said.

"And the trip to the convention?" Jane asked.

"I really did want to go to that, but it was also a great way to get you out of the house so they could do the work."

"Did you ask my mom about dimensions?" Jane asked Mike.

"I did. I didn't think she'd remember, though. You'd said that you and your dad always planned to do this, and I wanted it to be exactly as you planned," Mike said. "Luckily, Andie found those plans that you guys drew up."

"I can't believe you did all this in two days." Jane looked around the room again, this time taking in the details like the corner moldings on the bookshelves and the library ladder leaning against one of them.

"I tried to do as much as I could in my basement, and then we brought everything here," Mike said. "Had to work all night, but I think it came out pretty good."

"It's gorgeous!" Jane rushed over and kissed him on

the check. "Thank you all so much. I don't know what to say. What did I do to deserve this?"

"It was really Andie's idea," Mike said.

Jane looked at her sister, who blushed. "Not really. We both wanted to do something." Andie walked over and linked her arm through Jane's. "I just wanted a way to show that I appreciate that you've taken over running the inn. I know most of the burden rests on your shoulders."

"And I wanted to let you know that I appreciate how hard you work," Mike said. "I know I've been complaining about us not having enough time together, and that was selfish of me, so I wanted to do something to try to make up for that."

"Aw, you guys are the best!" Jane hugged them both then made her way around the room.

When she got to Bunny, Bunny said, "I didn't really do much, but this room will be perfect for the book club. Speaking of which, there's another surprise for you."

"There is?" Jane couldn't imagine how they would top the library surprise.

Bunny leaned in and whispered, "Turns out Mr. Smith is the author of the book club book."

"What?" That really was a surprise. "But I thought the author was Pat Jamison."

"He's here incognito. Didn't want to be mobbed by fans." Bunny laughed. "It's a long story, though we'll tell you about it later. For now, Brenda has been preparing some snacks, so let's party."

"*A*nd then Sam came and saved me from making a complete fool of myself." Bunny had just finished telling everyone about how she'd thought Mr. Smith was going to do away with his guest. She glanced over at Sam, who had been quiet the whole time she was telling the tale. Did he think she was just a silly old woman? His eyes still had that same sparkle of kindness.

"But how did you figure out he was the author?" Jane looked at the back of the book club book. "The photo is just really a shadow."

"I got curious and looked on the internet," Sam said.

"I should have thought of that. Guess I'm not that good of a detective." Bunny grimaced.

Sam patted her shoulder. "You did fine. Don't forget —you're just beginning, and I have years of experience. Besides, I would have thought the same as you, except I got curious about the book club. It was a fluke that I discovered his true identity, because I wouldn't have looked up the author of the book as part of the investigation."

"Well, maybe." That made Bunny feel a lot better.

"Enough about me. What's going on with you, Claire?" Claire had been pretty quiet, and Bunny sensed she had something on her mind.

"Oh, not much. Same old."

"How about the Beach Bones issue?" Maxi asked as she balanced a small plate with miniature sandwiches and tiny desserts.

"Oh, that. Well, there's been a development." Claire sighed.

"What?" Jane asked.

"It seems like Sandee is the other person selling Beach Bones."

Jane's eyebrows flew up. "You mean your ex-husband's wife?"

Claire pressed her lips together. "Yep."

"Well, that's an interesting development. What are you going to do?"

Claire shrugged. "I'm not sure. I mean, I could just pick another name, but somehow now that I know it's Sandee, that makes me want to keep it."

"It's not trademarked or anything, right?" Maxi asked.

"I had Tammi look, and she said no. The name is free and clear, but I wonder if I should just let it go so I don't have to deal with the drama," Claire said.

"Or maybe it would be a good way to get well-deserved revenge." Maxi popped a tiny quiche into her mouth and spoke around a mouthful. "She took your husband, and now you can take her dog biscuit name."

Claire laughed and put her hand over Rob's. "Well, turns out her taking my husband was a good thing. Now I have Rob."

"Awww… That's cute," Andie said. "I say you use the name and outsell the heck out of her."

Bunny stole a few glances at Sam as the others continued to discuss what Claire should do about the dog biscuits. She still felt awkward about how Sam had rushed in to save her from embarrassing herself in front of Mr. Smith. Afterward, she'd thanked him, and he'd assured her it was a mistake anyone could make, pointing out that he had also been suspicious. Still, Bunny couldn't help but feel weird about the whole thing.

Liz had invited them to the library reveal when they'd stumbled upon it the night before during the whole Mr. Smith debacle. Bunny wasn't really sure Sam would show up since he didn't know Jane very well, but she'd been happy to see him. He'd seemed happy to see her, too, but she really wasn't sure about that.

But now that the party was almost over, she wondered if she'd see Sam again. They didn't have the investigation as an excuse to meet. Should she invite him over for crossword night? No, that seemed contrived. At least she'd see him at book club, though she had kind of hoped they could become better friends than that.

She wondered what to do. Maybe going home and gardening was the best thing. The Mr. Smith investigation had been fun, but now it was over. Yeah, she'd made a few mistakes, but that wasn't going to stop her from investigating. She would learn from her mistakes and do better next time. *Maybe take on something a little less heavy than a murder. Perhaps a missing cat or dog?*

She could work her way up to getting a private investigator license. Either way, she planned to keep doing things that made her feel useful. And she didn't need Sam Campbell for that.

CHAPTER TWENTY-FIVE

*S*am stared down at his phone. It had been two days since the library reveal, and he'd thought Bunny might have texted him. The investigation was over, but surely, she might have something to say about the crossword puzzles. Maybe he should message her and invite her for a muffin at Sandcastles?

He hoped she didn't feel self-conscious over their presumptions toward Mr. Smith. It was only a fluke that Sam had discovered his true identity, and he'd agreed the man was acting suspicious. He'd already told her that. He hoped she didn't think he was just saying it to be nice.

He headed toward the garage to put away the paintbrush. He'd been doing more work on the house, making it his own. Not getting rid of Jean but just making her less prominent. She'd always be a part of his heart, but he had many years to live on his own, and he wanted them to be good ones.

A spot of shiny red color caught his eye. The cover had slipped off a corner of the Corvette. He went over and lifted it. The paint job was still pristine.

"Might as well take a look at her, eh?" he said to Dooley, who had trotted out behind him.

Dooley wagged his tail.

Sam slipped the cover off carefully and stood back. The top was down, and the leather seats still looked supple and comfortable. The paint was shiny. This time, instead of sad regrets, the sight of the car made his heart lift with happiness. He'd thought good times had died with Jean, but maybe not.

He pressed the button to open the garage door, then took the key from the peg on the wall and held his breath as he slid into the driver's seat and slipped it into the ignition. It started right up.

"Ready to go for a ride?" he asked Dooley.

The dog ran over to the passenger side. Sam opened the door, and Dooley jumped in.

"Maybe you'd better get in back. There might be a passenger that needs to sit there."

Dooley's ears stood up, and he glanced uncertainly at the back seat.

"Go ahead."

Dooley jumped in back, and Sam opened the garage

door and drove out. It was a little chilly for riding around in a convertible, but Sam relished the feeling of freedom and the wind in his hair. Well, what was left of it, anyway.

He took the scenic route, driving along the ocean. When he found himself turning into Bunny's neighborhood, he had a funny feeling in the pit of his stomach. Maybe this was a big mistake. She probably wasn't even home.

But she was home, and she was even outside, pruning the giant rose bush that grew at the corner of her house.

She turned as he pulled in. Her expression wasn't exactly as he'd hoped. She looked surprised but not happy to see him. *Oh no! This was a huge mistake.* She probably thought he was a foolish old man with a midlife crisis car. He wished he could back out and speed off, but it was too late. She was coming over to the car.

"Sam?" She peered into the car.

He gulped. "Want to go for a ride?"

She stared at him for a few more seconds, and he felt like sinking down into the seat and disappearing. Then her face cracked into a wide smile.

"I love convertibles! Of course I want to go for a ride! Whoop!" She ripped off her gloves and threw them onto the lawn. He got out to open the passenger door for her, but she practically vaulted into the car.

"You never told me you had a convertible," Bunny said.

"I haven't told you a lot of things. But I think we have plenty of time for that."

"I certainly hope so." She put her hand over his on the console, and he looked over at her. Her sparkling bright eyes were full of promise. He smiled and eased the car out of the driveway.

As he drove off, Dooley stuck his head between the two front seats. He put his chin on top of their hands, and all three of them knew it was the start of something good.

Meredith Summers / Annie Dobbs

Firefly Inn Series:

ABOUT THE AUTHOR

Meredith Summers writes cozy mysteries as USA Today Bestselling author Leighann Dobbs and crime fiction as L. A. Dobbs.

She spent her childhood summers in Ogunquit Maine and never forgot the soft soothing feeling of the beach. She hopes to share that feeling with you through her books which are all light, feel-good reads.

Join her newsletter for sneak peeks of the latest books and release day notifications:

https://lobsterbay1.gr8.com

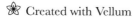 Created with Vellum

Made in United States
North Haven, CT
16 June 2023

37845883R00098